ECLIPSE

ECLIPSE

J. Bernlef

Translated by Paul Vincent

faber and faber

LONDON · BOSTON

First published in Great Britain in 1996
by Faber and Faber Limited
3 Queen Square London WC1N 3AU

Originally published in Dutch under the title *Eclips*
by E. Querido, Amsterdam, 1993

Phototypeset by Intype, London
Printed in England by Mackays of Chatham PLC, Chatham, Kent

A CIP record for this book is
available from the British Library

ISBN 0–571–17264–4

ECLIPSE

One

I have to turn right, off the road. The left-hand side of the world has disappeared, suddenly gone. So I have to turn right, into the dead straight canal. The rear bumper strikes the quayside with a loud crash. Then the sinking starts.

While I keep looking right I'm not particularly frightened, not paralysed with shock or panic as I was just now. I hear the water closing over the car roof, gurgling and sloshing. Then it begins to bubble in along the door seals and up through the floor in a muddy stream.

Water pouring in, slowly and yet quickly. I stare at it with a strange feeling in the right side of my head. As though the inside of my skull is starting to glow. Perhaps this is because the oxygen is gradually being replaced by the rising, murky water which is already above my knee (where is the other knee?).

Must get out. Get out. I will. A voice inside says, You'll get out! Just wait until the water has risen even higher and the pressure inside and outside is more or less equal.

I slide from behind the steering wheel on to the passenger seat. Meanwhile my thought processes continue, but somehow separately from me, as if functioning independently.

The water is lapping round my neck now. Diagonally beneath me I can see the silver door handle through the gloom. I bear down on the door with all my weight,

3

forcing the handle down. The door gives way. With eyes tight shut, I wriggle and squirm my way out through the half-open door.

For a moment I hang lopsidedly in the water, then I realize that I'm starting to rise. My right leg and arm move, thrash about, grab. I'm aware that I've broken the surface and open my eyes. There is the world! Nearby by a jetty juts into the water, low enough for me to catch hold of it in a moment and hoist myself up.

Now I know what I thought I felt just now: there is no longer anything there on the left-hand side; no world, but no body either. Yet from that direction, somewhere diagonally above me, I can hear the sound of cars zooming past. Luckily the right-hand side of my body hasn't deserted me. Indeed, I have the feeling it's stronger than usual. My right foot finds a hold on a post, my hand grabs an iron mooring ring somewhere in the middle of the jetty. They push and tug, the two of them, the leg and the arm. My ribcage scrapes across the rough wood. My head and my heart are pounding. I'm panting, the muddy water I've swallowed makes me cough. But I'm there! I get out, and inch by inch forces in the right side of my body pull me obliquely upwards. My right foot now rests on a protruding ledge, pushes against it and thrusts me flat on my face on the jetty. With a final effort I roll on to my back.

I smell the earthy water of the canal below me, hear the quacking of a duck, but can't locate the sound. I breathe deeply in and out. Above me there is a harsh blue sky full of clouds. The clouds drift past and then suddenly cease to exist. I follow them until they vanish into oblivion on my left. I close my eyes. My head rolls unbidden to the right.

I must have been asleep. Or unconscious, perhaps? It seems less light. My gaze is focused on the water's edge. Grass pollen, viper's bugloss, the last pink flower only half there, as if cut in half lengthways with a pair of scissors. Somewhere a cow moos and again I have no idea where that 'somewhere' is in relation to myself. Sounds no longer seem to come from a particular direction, to have a source. I sit up with difficulty, sliding across the planks on my one buttock. That's to say, the right-hand side of my body does; I can feel it.

On my left side there is nothing, my body stops halfway, although I can't work out exactly where the borderline is. I can't fathom it. Maybe later. For the moment I'll see if I can stand, can walk, haven't broken anything. No pain at all. Just a total absence of information about my left-hand side, but it must be somewhere.

Supporting myself on the palm of my right hand I get up, swaying slightly. Fields. And not far beyond them a high iron fence surrounding a site full of piles of buttercup-yellow crates. Perhaps there will be someone there, someone I can ask a few things.

I step on to the bank. Walking feels odd and unsteady. I totter as if I have a steering defect, keep pulling right, where it seems safer, as far as possible from that limit beyond which there is only sound.

I want to get to the section of fence in the sun, but my body (or what is left of it) tugs me its own way. Now the fence has gone – swallowed up.

If only there were a room, a chair, four walls around me. Instead of this space defined only by sounds, this disorientation gnawing at me. I feel like a fouled rudder.

Shall I lie down again? No, I must go on, keep moving, try to drag myself somewhere.

The grass suddenly changes to stone chippings under my feet. I look at the noise my shoe makes on the chippings, keep moving, haul myself along.

A concrete façade looms up, a wall full of square windows behind which there are steel desks. Suddenly I am right in front of it (although another part of the façade has now disappeared), without knowing exactly how I have covered the distance. The building has not come gradually closer in time, but has simply been placed in front of me. What has happened to the rest of it?

The desks are covered in folders and piles of papers. White telephones. On the walls calendars full of rows of severe black figures.

There is no one about. Out of office hours, Sunday perhaps? I walk cautiously towards the glass entrance doors. In the reception area an open newspaper lies on a table, too far away for the headlines to be legible. I turn round and carefully lower myself till my wet buttock feels the front step. An earthy canal smell rises from me, as though I had been underground for a time.

I must try and move along to the left, force my way in. Or is that whole concept meaningless now? (To tell the truth, I have a strong feeling that it is.)

To my astonishment I find that going left has become an impossibility. I can still think about left, a left-hand side, but it no longer has a reality. Or there's no longer a body there to take in the world. In any case, contact with it has become impossible. I suspect something is wrong inside me, has got dislodged perhaps. But exactly what has happened? And how did I wind up here, and why am I so wet?

Suddenly I burst into tears, something deep within me starts howling heart-rendingly, as uncontrollably as a wild animal. I bite hard into my hand, the one I still have the use of, in the hope that the pain will make the crying stop. It works. The sobbing subsides, and the shudders in the right-hand side of my chest gradually die away.

'What are you doing here?'

I jump. I scramble to my feet as quickly as I can, twirling round on my own axis.

I can hear a man's voice, but can't see a thing. I turn my head still further to the right. That voice again. Where from?

'What's your name?'

I turn further and further right until a hand grabs me from behind and jerks me round.

A tall, skinny lad in a dark uniform stands before me. He is wearing a cap with a shiny gold badge above the peak. Now I can see his thin lips moving, his small teeth, as he repeats his question. I can hear the impatience in his voice. So why don't I answer directly? What's stopping me?

'Well, you see, that's because I'm not exactly sure myself either at this moment, exactly. Either. Exactly. Mean exactly. Right, mean exactly. That.'

But that's not what I mean at all. That's why I'm glad he repeats his question, though the left-hand side of his face has disappeared and he gives me a sour look with what remains.

'Your name!' he shouts. 'Stop messing me about. I've got plenty else to do.'

'Yes, perhaps odd.'

Again one of those rambling openings.

'I beg no excuse,' I say. 'Occupation, birthplace. That. I know what you're driving at. My identity. Any time. Unfortunately I have no paper to record these facts on. You want to know my reputation, how I was named by my mother and father long ago.'

7

I feel myself blushing at all this floundering about, while I stand there helplessly. Like a fool. As though I'm soft in the head.

'My fame!' Again I falter. 'Something of that ilk or tenor, surely,' is the hesitant assumption I express to the young man, who is tugging at his left ear lobe (for me it's the right one). 'It has something to do with mud,' I add apologetically, more to myself than to the young man, who now gets so furious that he starts screaming.

'Oh yes,' he snarls. 'Your name is mud, of course.'

'Certainly. Name. Exactly! Why didn't I. . . ? That was it. Yes, yes. So near and yet so far. Obviously.'

'Windbag. Taking the piss, are we?' He grabs me and pushes me ahead of him. Out of the corner of my right eye I can see his hand, which has my arm in an iron grip. The rest of him is in a kind of no man's land from where I can hear him puffing and panting beside me.

'Bloody hell. You stink to high heaven, mate. Don't let me catch you here again!'

He shoves me out into the world (fortunately to the right), down an asphalt road, along which I start stumbling at a jog.

I stop beneath a row of rustling poplars. Best to lie down here at the side of the road for a bit. On the soft verge. Think things over. Fortunately I can still do that.

Something terrible has happened. The world seems to have eaten half of me away. Again I start weeping uncontrollably. My hand clutches at tall stalks of grass. What's happened to my other hand?

Something is wrong with my speech too. And what about my name? No idea where it can have got to; surely I must have had one once? Without a name you're unfit for human society. The young man was right on that count, although in other ways he struck me as pretty stupid. Impatient like most young people. He asked simple questions, to which I still had no answer; I knew the answer but couldn't give it.

I listen to the leaves above me, swishing and whispering. I mustn't lie here too long in these wet clothes. I must keep going, get away from this area, which is obviously private, find a safer place. Once I have found that I can start remembering myself. My name for a start. The one your mother called from the window. When it was time to eat. Come on in! I can remember her voice. It was light and had a way of breaking as it became shriller. Come on in! What then? Come on, what did my mother call me?

The road suddenly stops. I see a fence and climb over it. At least that's what I mean to do. Halfway there my body refuses to stay upright: it lacks internal balance and an overall view. I fall over and roll on to the ground, and in a flash I see the world spinning past in close-up, and again space encloses me completely for a second.

I scramble to my feet and repeat the experiment. Slowly I turn right on my own axis. A farmhouse and, in front of the farmyard, a row of pollarded willows give way to a semicircular shed made of sheet metal. Then a tall white building and a flagpole on the square, close-cropped lawn in front of it. Slowly I turn further. Little by little a collection of allotments appears. Huts built of old planks by the side of flower or vegetable beds. No one about. Then the farmhouse comes back into my field of vision. So it has definitely been there the whole time, in a fixed place. That means it's my fault, not the world's, that I can't keep it in focus. The world exists apart from me, as a continuous whole. Absurd that I should feel the need to prove it to myself, that I should feel so relieved at discovering this self-evident fact. Absurd! But I would have to keep turning round in order to experience it as a whole. In that way I would never get anywhere. So I must make a choice.

Again I slowly turn round on the spot until the allotments appear, the wooden huts, the plots and flowerbeds. They strike me as more friendly and welcoming than the farmhouse with the row of pollarded willows or the tall white building with its austere lawn and flagpole. I walk on until I get to the middle of the allotments (by my own estimate at least). It's safer in the middle than at the edge. Most of the huts are locked, but on one of them the padlock is hanging loose; I can simply take it off.

Inside it smells of sawdust. I sit down at the table and look through a small, dirty window covered in brown fly stains.

The hut in Koog aan de Zaan had a window like that. Could I be there? At Old Daan's. Old Daan the baker? So I know other names, other people's names, but not my own. But I'll get it back. I seem to remember that I don't have a very complicated name. Just four letters. Two identical vowels enclosed by two consonants. Something like Daan, but different. And a rather longer surname: two syllables. I can see them in my mind's eye like grey smudges.

In a corner near the door is a large pile of newspapers. I get up and take a few off the top, walk backwards and spread them out on the table. I leaf through a paper as far as the death announcements, which I recognize by their heavy black edges. Inside the black boxes there are names, names of the dead. When I turn a page it vanishes, as though somebody on my left was taking it out of my hands. I wish I still had a left hand.

There is nothing wrong with my eyes and the characters are bold and black. But I can't read them. I can make out groups of letters, but they no longer communicate anything. They have become separate black signs, clustered in groups. Together they form sentences – a narrative. I know how it works, but something or someone is preventing me from applying that knowledge to the text in front of me. I push the newspaper to the extreme right-hand corner of the table, hoping that the meaning will get through to me better from there, but that doesn't help. The layout of the paper seems familiar, though. I close my eyes tight and immediately open them again, but the newspaper remains a mysterious piece of printed paper.

A muddy stench fills the inside of the hut. It's me. It's my clothes. I must take them off. I must find some water to wash them in. I get up and turn slowly to the right. The pile of newspapers disappears so abruptly that I have the greatest difficulty in continuing to believe it is still somewhere in the room, on a table which has vanished too. Now I see a draining board, but no tap. These clothes will have to come off in any case.

That's easier thought than done. On my right side it's not too bad, but the left-hand side of my shirt and trousers only exists in my mind. Only by concentrating very hard do I finally succeed in peeling the clothes off that side of me; there's no feeling in it. The white shirt is covered in mud stains and streaks of waterweed. My grey trousers are black. With the clothes over my arm, I finally shuffle out in my underpants, sideways like a crab, on my one bare foot.

When I get outside I see that it's growing dark. In the

11

distance I hear a lorry changing gear. I stumble through an allotment. Now and then I twist round to hold on to the notion of surroundings. A pump comes into view; an old-fashioned pump with a handle. I shuffle towards it, in as straight a line as possible. It's cold. Before I start washing the clothes, I check through my trouser pocket, inspecting it carefully. Empty. A habit from the past, I can tell by the practised movement of my right hand. I suppress the thought of a left-hand pocket.

To make the pump work I have to let go of the clothes. In the hollow of my hand I feel the round iron knob of the short handle. A campsite in the middle of a wood. There was one there too. I was only small. I had to stand on tiptoe and push against the underside of the handle with my whole weight to make the pump catch, just like now. First a few dry strokes, then a meagre trickle of water, followed suddenly by a broad gush.

First I wash the parts of me I can still recall. Halfway across my chest my rubbing hand loses hold and hastily withdraws under my right armpit. I hang first the shirt and then the trousers over the curved top of the pump. Perhaps they'll get a little cleaner. Sometimes a bit of clothing slides off the top of the pump on to the drain grating and I have to start all over again. I try to involve my left hand in the work, but I have no idea where it is.

I squeeze the sodden clothes with one hand, sniffing them. They still stink, but not quite as much. I have difficulty in finding my way to the hut, even doubt its existence for a moment.

There's no light. No bed. I shall have to lie down on the ground. I improvise as good a bed as I can with the pile of newspapers. I remember I used to tuck newspapers under my shirt before going skating, next to my bare chest. They kept the wind out, the biting north-east wind which always swept across the polders in winter. I slide between the crackling layers of newspaper, turning carefully on to my stomach. Pitch blackness. For a little while I'm at peace. I'm alone with a few thoughts slowly dissolving like flakes at the onset of sleep, with the high-pitched singing sound of skate blades across an endless, desolate expanse of ice; left, right, right, left, fainter and fainter, further and further away from me.

I'm woken by sunlight on my cheek. I'm lying on the old newspapers, on a wooden floor. The paper rustles as I move. I sit up. I stare at the letters on my lap. Meaningless. I raise my right shoulder and in my mind, somewhere I cannot fix in space, something moves with it that was once called my left shoulder, or at least was somewhere thereabouts.

I shuffle over to the table at the window. My shirt and trousers are lying in front of me in a wet bundle. I must hang them out to dry on the section of the brown-stained fence outside that exists for me.

It is still early, misty. I remember coming here. A hut in a group of allotments, but how and where from? It's all just happened, but still I can't retrieve it. Not in the way I used to remember the day before; images, conversations, whose content and tone I could often recall almost word for word.

Once outside with the clothes, I have to turn round a few times before I catch sight of the dark brown fence again. Or is this a different brown fence? I shuffle towards it down a flagstone path, holding the clothes. I shake them out, separating the shirt from the trousers, and with one hand fold them clumsily over the top of the fence. Then I see the old man standing on the other side. He's staring at me as though he has seen a ghost.

'Dallo, gir,' I say. When I hear what I come out with, my hand grabs hold of the fence in alarm.

An old man in blue overalls and a check shirt. Stubbly sunken cheeks. A multi-coloured handkerchief knotted at the corners on his head. His pale eyes watch me suspiciously, and now he puts a hand to his right ear, as though he hasn't heard me properly. Perhaps he wants to give me a second chance. I open my mouth and he takes a step forward between the two narrow beds full of bamboo canes. Strips of silver paper attached to the canes rattle when a brief gust sweeps along the ground. His figure disappears partially from my field of vision.

'Gents I salute you,' I say.

He gapes, grabs one of the braces holding up his overalls.

'Foreigner, I suppose?' His nasal voice is younger and more high-pitched than his appearance would suggest.

'Certainly not, from no stranger,' I hear my voice say, the one that speaks on my behalf and keeps getting things slightly wrong. I can feel tears of helplessness welling up.

The old man doesn't dare come any closer. His heavy white eyebrow twitches nervously. Then, with a hand that comes from nowhere, he makes a dismissive gesture across his face, turns abruptly and walks – whole once more – towards the open door of a low greenhouse shaped like a frame tent. A gesture that implies he has only imagined me. I feel tears running down my cheeks. The smell of earth and potatoes keeps me on my feet, though I should prefer to lie down here, let my wrecked body flop to the ground.

I can see the old man in his greenhouse. He holds a

watering can out in front of him like a weapon. Then I turn round. No conversation is possible. The sun is shining on my bare shoulder. Luckily the fence is between him and me, so that he can't see that I am almost naked (or should I say half-naked?). I can only hope that he really has forgotten me, and doesn't fetch someone. If more people were to get involved I'd be completely at a loss. My thoughts go haywire the moment I express them, in sentences I don't mean to say.

I put my shoes outside the door. The warm air penetrates the wooden shack. I feel it soothing my skin.

I swivel round and look about me. No books anywhere. What good would books be to me anyway? I can't read them. Then I see a contraption of some sort. It's next to the steel draining board on a wooden shelf. A thin steel rod sticks out of it and it has two shiny silver knobs. Not knowing what it is, I go towards it, pick it up and take it over to the table, which I find only after turning round twice (must be because I'm so nervous). My heart is in my mouth. I feel the aluminium object from all sides. The word for the thing is on the tip of my tongue. My hand twiddles one of the knobs. When a voice suddenly comes out of the contraption I let go of it in fright. Then I smile and stroke the cool metal. Of course, of course, it's just a transistor radio. It was as if the object, the radio, gave its name back to me the moment I touched it. As if the right word was stored not in my brain but in my fingertips.

'A broadcasting station,' my voice whispers. 'An authorized transmitter.'

I go on stroking the smooth radio and listening to a reassuring male voice talking about the composer Joseph Haydn. His words find their way in as they always have done. I nod, full of blissful comprehension.

Then the music starts. A piano. Suddenly I can feel my left ear! I take hold of it with a perfect aim. Where has it come from so suddenly? With my finger I massage the tingling edge of the ear, the lobe. My left ear is back!

I lean heavily on my elbow, listening to the music. The tingling continues as far as my neck. It's as if the music is drawing the outline of that part of my body in space with a light pen. The image of my left-hand side seems to be returning, especially now that the music speeds up in a joyful cascade of notes. Suddenly my left knee strikes the underside of the tabletop, knocking the radio over. With the music gone, my knee, shoulder and neck also fade, until only the slight tingling in the edge of my ear persists, like an after-image on the retina.

I set the radio upright and twiddle the knobs, but the music can't be found. A woman's voice announces a programme on flower arranging and gives the time. Ten-thirty. The tingling persists.

On my left-hand side a jewel has emerged from the surrounding nothingness. I clutch it tenderly with my right hand. I still don't dare look to my left, but I know that it's no longer just emptiness there, I can feel something again. So I let go of the ear. I know now that it will stay where it is, on the left-hand side of my skull, the same as everyone else's. I convince myself that it won't disappear. If there were a mirror in here, I'd be able to check my body, see exactly what's wrong with it. Yet I shan't go hunting for one. The idea of a mirror disgusts me.

Cautiously I fiddle with the radio again. I listen to a sports programme for a while. Conversations flow automatically and effortlessly. I can follow them at the speed at which they are spoken, but there's no way I could speak so fast myself. Because I can only react to what I hear in thoughts, not in words, the words coming out of the radio seem more penetrating, louder and find their way in without meeting any resistance. I can't respond. Powerless, I am subjected to other people's speech.

I search until I find some music again. A choir of high-pitched boys' voices. 'High on the yellow wagon,' they sing.

'I ride o'er hill and dale,' I sing along softly. The music evokes something from the past and in exactly the right words. When the song is over, I turn the radio off. I gently hum an old children's song. Hushaby, hushaby. My voice buzzes like an insect through the wooden hut.

If you can sing, sing along! That album was always open on the piano in our house. My mother's small hands, which could scarcely span an octave, played the accompaniment almost shyly while my sister Hanna and I stood on either side of the black piano stool. Hanna had very dark eyes and hair. I was twelve when she was born, an afterthought. I can remember a photograph in which I am standing staring in astonishment at a baby with bushy black hair. Your father used to be as dark as that, I can hear my mother say. Hanna. Where has she got to? I can see her quite clearly in front of me as a child, but after that nothing. Yet she must still be alive somewhere, grown up.

I put my hand on the radio. A prop. Music gives me room to manoeuvre. I must keep it close to me. Clutching the radio in my right hand I shuffle outside.

It's warmer than inside. In a corner of the allotment there is a wicker chair with a stained seat. I sit down on it with the radio on my lap. In the anonymous space on my left-hand side a woman's voice explodes, shrill and cheerful. 'Trees!* Coffee!'

Trees. That's almost my own name. I'm sure of it. 'Keef,' says my mouth. 'Kee-oo.' Then I have it: Kees! 'Keef,' says my voice again. No, Kees. 'Keef,' my voice keeps insisting aloud.

The sun warms me, dries my underpants. I look up into the cloudless sky, which seems closer. Or rather not closer, but part of the day. Like it should, like it must always have been, in the past. I look up again, smiling, almost trusting in all that clear blue around me.

'Keef,' I whisper. I've got my name back. Kees. I'm sure my name is Kees. I get up. Suddenly I am overcome with hunger. Slowly, getting my bearings, I begin turning. Then I tense up. The radio! It has vanished from my world. Quickly I turn right round. There it is again. I kneel down and pick it up. Light as a feather.

Radios used to be much bigger and heavier; made of wood and bakelite, a loudspeaker in the middle with a moquette screen behind curved bars. When Dad put on the radio you could hear the sound slowly growing. At the back you could see the valves starting to glow through gaps in the cover. We sat round the table and listened to a radio play. Paul Temple, with that opening theme tune, dynamic and at the same time menacing. I try to remember it, pursing my lips, but it won't come out. Too long ago, I think, too far away.

My stomach rumbles. I hunt through the right-hand side of the world, twisting my neck as far as possible, but can't see anything edible. There are no shops here. When my clothes are dry I must get going, and try to find something to eat.

* Pronounced somewhat like 'trace'.

When I'm back at the hut with my dry clothes and trying to get dressed, I suddenly remember the radio. With my trousers round my ankles I stagger outside. Fortunately the radio appears at once. I take it inside with me, put it on the visible side of the table and twiddle the knobs in vain. Of course, first switch it on at the side! The hissing reassures me; it's still working. When I hear music – lively music (jazz?) – I wait expectantly to test my theory. I think of the left-hand side of my body, my leg, my hand which, together with the two right-hand limbs, should now be hurrying to help me get dressed perfectly. My ear starts tingling again, then my shoulder jerks and the left leg thrashes about wildly in its trouser leg and almost knocks me over. I rock to and fro to the rhythm of the music, bend over and see two hands hitching up my trousers, co-operating as though it were the most natural thing in the world. I don't know how quickly I have to button up the shirt. I must make sure I have finished before the music stops.

I sit down panting. Here and there I can feel there is a button in the wrong buttonhole, but generally things appear to be more or less in order. The stench hasn't quite gone.

New tunes the whole time, all similar, but so much the better. I think I can now risk standing up to feel my whole body, to move in time with this music. Perhaps I'll be able to.

Hips swaying, I move about the hut and suddenly turn left. Exactly the same feeling I used to have in the dancing class. The Martin School of Dancing. What big feet you have, said the dancing teacher. Yes, that's true. Big, bare feet, and quite dirty too. My shoes must be somewhere. I take hold of the radio, still playing, and it acts as a compass.

I step outside and there they are, waiting for me right by the door. Still a bit damp, but wearable. No need to tie the laces. Maybe later when they're completely dry. No I've a better idea. I take the shoes back in with me and put them on the table. With my other, left hand, made visible and tangible by music, I put the radio, still playing, next to them. I have to laugh at how smoothly and quickly everything is suddenly progressing. I pull the laces out of the shoes, tie them together, run the dark brown cord under the retractable handle of the transistor, and tie the ends in a double knot. Carefully I lift the radio by the cord and bend my neck. I push the cord over my head. The radio is now hanging against my chest just below my chin. I walk cautiously, first left then right, across the wooden floor. I can't say that my entire body is back where it should be, but what was just a vague memory of a wholeness once possessed has now rematerialized, in a technical sense at least, to the rhythm of this blaring brass-band music. Then I hear a voice. It's the voice of the old man in the overalls, sharp and nasal, coming from what must be the doorway.

'What the hell are you doing in there, tramp!'

I turn round. To the left. As if on skates, I sweep elegantly towards him, pushing him effortlessly aside. To judge by the noise behind me I think the old man stumbles and falls, but I haven't time to look. 'Police,' I hear him yelling. 'I'll call the police!'

Majestically, with head held high, I jog away from the allotments, at one with the wailing guitars under my chin.

It may just be me, but all these office blocks, factory buildings and sheds separated by patches of waste ground or mounds of sand deposited as slurry, where the first weeds are already poking through again, seem to have only just been put here. While I wasn't looking. There seems to be no plan behind their relative positions. Now and then I am passed by sand trucks or delivery vans which sound their horns loudly. Thanks to the music from the radio they no longer emerge from nowhere but simply approach from the left-hand world.

Through windows I can see people everywhere bent over their work. Doing things that I have a clear view of through the glass. Girls in white overalls sit in a line at a long packing table. I stop for a moment and watch the lightning movements with which their fingers put sweets into boxes as they talk and laugh together without looking up.

Signs with letters on them are fixed to the roofs and the fronts of the factory buildings and offices, some of them neon, pointlessly lit in the bright sunshine. The letters present themselves, form words, probably the names of products. I try not to look at them. I pass a high iron fence behind which hundreds of identical cars are lined up one behind the other in long rows, by colour. Metallic grey, grass green, navy blue. They have no number plates. At the end of the fence there is an opening with a wooden gatekeeper's hut next to it. As I walk past I see a young man loosening his tie with one hand and pouring coffee from a white thermos flask with the other. I walk past, feeling ravenous. Further on, a little way off the road, there is a lopsided barn. In front of it a goat grazes, tethered to a peg in the ground by a long rope. The radio on my chest is playing an accordion tune. I walk over to the barn without really knowing why. Perhaps because the collapsed wooden wall and the dull red tile roof inspire confidence, don't repel me like the glass façade and concrete walls. The goat comes with me a little way. When it can go no further, it gives a little bleat and turns round. I look into the barn through a cracked window. Piles of planks lie on a concrete floor. In one corner sit three black oil drums. I walk round the barn. Behind it alder trees rustle. In among their trunks are two squashed cola cans and an empty packet of biscuits. I pick up the wrapping paper and sniff it. It must have been lying here for some time, smells of grass. I drop it. Beyond the alders a pond. Two mallards sprint away over the water, flapping their wings.

Suddenly the music stops. I turn the dial nervously, but can't find music anywhere. My body immediately tugs to the right, and the left-hand side again merges with my surroundings.

In front of me seagulls soar above a hilly area. Beneath my chin a woman's voice rattles away in French. I turn the radio off and in the silence hear my shoe shuffling through the tall grass. Nowhere can I see any more factories or sheds. I must think about a direction. I stop and slowly turn on my own axis. The industrial estate is in the distance. I don't want to go back. Nothing there but people working. No food. When I turn further and am almost back in my original position, I see an old oak tree with a broad crown. Under it a black car with no wheels. A wooden board hangs from the door handle. On it a signwriter has drawn a cup of coffee or soup. Steam spirals upwards from the cup in pale wisps of colour. Under the cup of coffee or soup there are some words and a red arrow pointing to the right, towards a green hut a little further on. A vaguely familiar green flag flutters above the door. Something connected with drinking. Cautiously I establish my position in relation to the hut – it seems to be about two hundred yards ahead – and then begin shuffling sideways in a straight line over the bumpy ground towards the door with the flag over it. A vague smell of rotting rubbish wafts towards me, so that I retreat instinctively, have to stop and turn right round again, until the hut is immediately in front of me once more. It's closer now. I'm making progress. Several times I stumble in shallow depressions hidden under the tall grass. The radio, rocking to and fro, rubs against my shoulder. At one of the windows of the hut (at least I assume there is more than one) I can make out someone in a hat. The figure at the window seems to be watching my approach intently and without moving. I turn my head so that the figure vanishes.

On opening the hut door I am met by the flicker of neon over a formica-topped counter. Behind the sloping glass frontage I see rissoles and sausages in breadcrumbs next to dishes of sliced meat. My mouth waters. There is no one behind the counter. From the area that I can't see I hear a hoarse woman's voice calling 'Jannie'. A young girl in a grey sweater with letters on it enters my available field of vision.

'Jannie's not here,' she says. Only then does she see me. I realize she's alarmed: I must look pretty dishevelled. The girl has painted her lips the same bright red as the short nails of her fat fingers. Nervously she passes one hand through her shoulder-length straw-blond hair. Then she says something to me.

'What can I get you?'

'Let me, from the outset, issue forth a statement,' I say. 'Finances have gone astray. You know, bills, debits, invoices, proofs of payment, everything through the bank, sometimes automatically. Now it's like this.'

I slap my belly with my hand. The girl stares at me and then shakes her head slowly.

23

'Comprehension difficult,' I agree. 'Something has taken place up here.'

I tap the right-hand side of my skull. 'Everything is properly arranged inside, but it won't come out of the sluice gates any more, you know.'

The girl now turns to someone in the part of the snack bar which is invisible to me.

'If you ask me, this customer's not very well, Toos.'*

She waits for an answer from the direction of the person she has spoken to. Cautiously I turn right round.

A large woman wearing an enormous hat decorated with artificial flowers is sitting at a table in one of the two windows. On the chairs next to and opposite her are plastic bags crammed with old newspapers, pieces of wood and PVC piping of various thicknesses and lengths. The woman has a narrow pointed face. Her brown hair pushes out from under her hat in tiny curls. An army greatcoat with a double row of brass buttons comes down almost to her ankles. On her small feet she has black lace-up boots, their toes curled up. Frowning and screwing up her green eyes she regards me thoughtfully. I slap my belly again and open my mouth, but she silences me with an imperious movement of her wrist.

'May well be, dear,' she says. 'But give the poor sod a ham roll on me. He's got no money. I understood that much.'

She beckons me over to her table. 'Just you put those bags down,' she says.

I lower the plastic bags carefully to the ground and sit down opposite her. I'm grateful to hear that she has at least made an effort to understand me. Again I tap my right temple.

* Pronounced somewhat like 'toas(t)'.

24

'Of course, you've gone off your head,' she agrees. 'Dear me, you're not the only one. When you look around you. They're all as dotty as each other.'

'No,' I say. 'Not at the level of imbecility. Only thing I can't do is in-house editing of text. That's the snag. The last set of proofs lost, so lots of mistakes are left in.'

'Well, you still don't seem quite right in the head to me.' She gives me a motherly pat on my remaining arm. 'Who on earth walks about with a radio round his neck?'

I nod. That certainly must be a strange sight, but how am I to explain it to her? I put out my hand.

'Keef,' I say.

'Well, Kees,' she says. 'Your name is Kees. Well, my name's Toos.' She laughs and I can see that she has a couple of top teeth missing.

I jump when a plate with a ham roll on it is suddenly pushed into my field of vision. I tuck in greedily. I stuff everything into the right side of my mouth for fear the food will fall out or leak in some other way on the left-hand side. To my surprise the roll disappears in two mouthfuls. It looked like quite a large roll.

'Would you like another one?' says the woman, and as she leans forward comes completely into view.

'It's gone,' I say helplessly.

'Here,' she says and shoves the dish with the half-eaten roll on it in front of my nose. My right hand grabs it, stuffs it into my mouth, as though I'm afraid it will disappear again.

'Well, he's hungry all right,' says the woman to the young girl, whom I can now hear but no longer see.

'Yes, I know what it's like walking around with an empty stomach,' Toos says in a familiar tone. 'And I suppose you haven't got anywhere to live either?'

I shake my head as I eat.

25

'I left,' I say. 'And suddenly all my bridges, madam. Nothing left. No notion of direction or place.'

'As long as he's not on drugs,' I hear the girl say anxiously, as she stands noisily washing cups.

'Doesn't look the type to me,' says the woman called Toos. One can't tell what her figure is like under the army greatcoat, or her age for that matter. Forty, fifty, she could be either.

'Or a loony then,' the girl's voice continues behind me. 'They all walk the streets quite freely these days, it seems. I'd be careful if I were you, Toos.'

Toos shrugs her shoulders. 'What does loony mean? I've seen crazier ones than this.'

Then she gets up. She points to the plastic bags next to me on the ground.

'Come on, Kees,' she says. 'We're going.'

I pick up the plastic bags and keep a close watch on her. I mustn't lose sight of her. Perhaps she has a place to stay, a room, four walls within which I can sort my thoughts out.

'Can feel OK,' I say, 'but it doesn't come out of the mouth. Still, congratulations. No, many, many thinks. Do you mean what I feel?'

'Come on,' she says impatiently, as though speaking to a dawdling child.

When we get outside I walk by her side so I can see her the whole time, so she can't suddenly disappear on my left.

'Only upon the one side,' I say by way of explanation. 'I can't turn about any more. Blocked. Do you feel?'

'Of course,' the woman next to me says good-naturedly.

26

The road now becomes sandy soil overlaid with sheets of iron, the sort sometimes used for lorries to drive across building sites. She points to a row of houses under construction. Above the roofs the end of a yellow crane effortlessly defies gravity. To begin with something like that would have surprised me, but I'm already so used to my fragmented field of vision that I know the block of the crane must be somewhere, in another world, I'm inclined to think.

'Houses galore here,' she says. 'Until they're finished, that is. And when they're finished you look for another one.'

She's now walking straight across the soft sand towards the terrace of low houses. There are piles of stones and bags of cement everywhere. I walk behind her, lugging the plastic bags.

It must be afternoon, the sun is already low over the blue-grey roofs of the windowless houses. I'm beginning to feel hungry again.

'The back terrace,' I hear her say. 'They've already got water.'

With considerable effort we step from the soft sand over a high threshold on to the bare concrete floor of a room with empty window frames. Here and there bunches of electric wires stick out of the wall. Toos puts her bags against the roughly plastered wall. I put mine next to them and turn off the radio. She walks through the doorless rooms in her long army coat, hands on hips, inspecting the accommodation. In what will eventually be the bathroom she turns on a tap. A powerful jet of water rushes into the white washbasin. Something which is perfectly normal, but which sends her into ecstasy. She turns to me. 'What did I tell you?' She grins. I nod.

Through the bathroom window I look out over a hilly patch of grassland. I see a man watching his dog disappear into reeds fringing a pool. Behind me I can hear the tap running. The dog re-emerges from the reeds and shakes itself dry. Then it stops and listens for a moment, legs straight and ears pricked. In the distance a narrow chimney smokes. The dog bends its head, sniffs the ground briefly and trots into oblivion. If I were to turn to the right I might be able to pick him up again from a different angle. I don't, I let him go. I am looking at the world like a picture book, with someone else turning the pages. The water in the puddles scattered over the building site looks black. For the first time my body feels like a prison from which I would like to escape. To turn right round to the left. Without music I don't dare. Then I hear her voice.

'Hey, are you just going to stand there?'

When I cautiously turn a hundred-and-eighty degrees she is standing in front of me, naked.

She is drying herself with a black dress embroidered here and there with silver leaves. She rubs the dress between her thighs a couple of times without the slightest embarrassment. She's not bad looking. But even now that she's naked I can't tell her age, or the sort of life that must have preceded her presence here. And I too seem to be simply here without any prehistory. My eyes fill with tears.

She comes towards me, presses her body against mine and strokes my back. I can feel her hand move from my right shoulder blade across my back and then disappear without trace.

'Come on,' she whispers. 'There's nothing to cry about.'

I shake my head and push her gently away.

She shakes out the dress and steps into it while she looks at me sideways from beneath her loosely hanging hair.

'You're a strange one,' she says. 'You're gawping as though you're in a museum. Or do you think I'm ugly or something?'

Again I shake my head. I can feel how the muscles round my mouth are trying to form a word. The word 'beautiful', which comes out as 'dutiful'.

'Beautiful, I expect you mean.'

I smile. I'm not getting the words right but she still understands me. I go over to her, but at that second she bends down towards her boots and vanishes. I stand stock-still in the white-tiled room with my arm outstretched.

I'm still alarmed by this sudden disappearance of bits of matter which an instant ago were there, and looked so solid that there seemed to be no reason at all to doubt their existence. It's as if I'm in the company of a malevolent magician who at any moment can rob me of pieces of my own reality. So I stand there for a long time with my arm outstretched, adjusting to what's just happened.

And when I've made yet another complete about turn she is standing in the passageway with the greatcoat over her arm. She beckons and disappears through a doorway. Once I used to know the person was still there. I still do. And yet I hear myself calling her name in panic. Doos! Doos! Invisibly present – somewhere – she calls my name in reply.

I follow her voice blindly. In a corner of the room which suddenly detaches itself as quite separate from the rest of the space, she is sitting on an old grey blanket under a window opening. I sit next to her in the dusk with the absent part of my body turned away from her.

I look at her, smile uncertainly. Perhaps that awakens motherly feelings in her. She pulls me on to my back and spreads the greatcoat over me. I stare at a round black hole in the ceiling. My mouth opens and shuts, tasting the words of my thoughts without being able to speak them. The coat smells musty, of peat dust, fen soil or something of that sort overlaid with the hint of some sickly sweet perfume.

'In oilier times, long past,' I hear my voice orating in the dark. 'That must have been.' I falter.

Been. Have. The words have a way of detaching themselves from the sentence, becoming independent and hence no longer meaning anything. Sense and sentence. Once the two things were inextricably linked. Now I wonder which came first: sentence or sense?

'They've really given you a hard time.' She strokes my good cheek.

'Something wrong,' I say. 'Has gone a long way away.'

'It'll be all right.' She gets up and has gone.

I close my eyes. Then I feel more certain of a fixed place on earth, stretched out here on this concrete floor. In the distance I can hear the rustle of plastic. A distance which may be anywhere.

When she is (not 'comes') back she has a hunk of bread in her hand. She tears off a piece and gives it to me, sinking her teeth into what's left. I sniff the bread before I start eating.

'Bread,' I suddenly say. 'Bread!'

Of course she doesn't understand why that makes me laugh so much, I'm so happy that I've picked up the thread, however briefly, the thread between me and things. But immediately afterwards it goes wrong again.

'Keef. Before Keef too. I mean when I was still a mother-sayer. Bread.'

She answers with a question. Obviously couldn't follow me this time.

'What do you do? Have you got a job, Kees? Or do you just scratch about, like me?'

She is trying to get me on to a different track, but I can't do it. Not before I have repeated the word mother-sayer a couple of times. Of course I mean mother, back then, that I was there back then, but can't feel it any more (though I know it). But however clearly I can think it, it comes out just as garbled. Once in my mouth language takes over from me and tumbles out in aimless sequences of words. Perhaps if I had the radio. I sit up, but she holds me back.

'What do you want? You're not going, are you?'

'Music,' I say. 'Tubes, knobs and then that suddenness, those sounds from that shiny thing. I want that.'

'Let me get it,' she says. 'I know my way around here better than you.'

A moment later she appears with the transistor. She turns a knob. A Beethoven string quartet fills the room. She's about to go on turning the dial, but I shake my head violently.

'Do you really like that sloppy stuff?' She turns the dial back with a sigh until the reception is clear again. My left leg starts jerking, tingling intensely. My toes emerge somewhere down in the depths, for the time being still separate from the foot they are attached to. I move them, half sit up and try to have a look, but it's already too dark to see them.

'It reminds me of funerals, that kind of music,' she says with a sigh. She lies down again and pulls the greatcoat towards her a little.

My mouth moves, but doesn't speak. My muscles use the cadence of the interweaving violins, clearing the way for sentences already thought up that suddenly cross my lips effortlessly. 'Something has happened to me. It's as though the left side of my body has gone. It's just that with music it reappears, and I can speak like I used to.'

'Everything's in its place, as far as I can tell,' she says cheerfully in the darkness. 'Nothing to get worried about.'

You can't explain something like this to anyone else.

Then she suddenly turns off the radio.

'Let's get some kip.'

I try to protest, to go on enjoying the presence of my whole body, the inner image of arms, legs, ribcage and back which I wasn't even aware of before. Now that I've lost parts of my body, I feel that muscles and nerves must have some kind of independent consciousness which transmits the image of the body as a totality, so that you can always act on that assumption, a consciousness which is separate from what I call my 'self'. Or used to. And that consciousness has lost part of its memory.

'No,' she says firmly and pushes my hand away. 'If a night-watchman comes by we'll be in for it. Turn it off.'

In the dark I dare to turn very slowly on to my left side. I feel my body's comforting resistance to the stone floor. Flesh, bones, which are still there, even now the music has gone, which announce their presence and gently continue tingling. It was like this when you had been ice-skating and were sitting at home in front of the stove; a delicious pain turning into languor glowed through your whole body, as if you were slowly melting, huddled on a chair by the stove, waiting for the mug of hot chocolate with eagerly outstretched hands.

When I wake, stiff as a board, the toes in my left foot can still be felt somewhere out there. They haven't gone back to that world without space and time that I can only imagine as a concept: 'absence'. But in fact that word doesn't mean anything. It describes something that by definition is inconceivable. Something like one's own death.

And now, as I gradually sit up, I observe that the fingertips of my left hand are also tingling in the same way. Most of my left side is still dumbstruck, but the fingers and toes seem to have cautiously returned. I sit on the grey blanket – Toos must have taken her greatcoat with her – and listen to my body. The electric tingling seems to have come from nowhere. It's simply there, in the space occupied by my body, like a row of flickering lights in an otherwise dark night (if only I could draw my situation!). The vague contours of a row of toes at the bottom of the page and at the top the fingertips with the shiny beginning of the nails. In between, blank paper, the word absence.

It must still be early. Uncertain light enters through the window opening. Somewhere, to judge by the sound not far away, I can hear Toos shuffling about. I get up and hang my radio round my neck. I'm not yet ready for a confrontation with the left side of the world, although my toes and fingertips are already there. I turn on my own axis and shuffle in the direction of the crinkling plastic. When I go through the doorway into another room, Toos is just putting on her big flowered hat. Her red mouth contrasts sharply with all those pale blue, pink and sea-green flowers of taffeta and silk. When she sees me her hands coyly release the brim of the hat.

'What do you think of Mrs Morningstar?'

I'm not ready to talk yet and just nod. My hips are hurting from the night on the bare floor. My hips? Yes, the left hip now makes itself known too, its outlines defined by painful stabs inside my frame.

Toos picks up the army greatcoat, which is lying on the floor on top of the plastic bags by the wall, and hoists herself into it.

'Come on,' she says. 'We must be off before the builders get here.'

I point to the row of plastic bags full of newspapers, bits of wood and PVC piping.

She glances at them casually and then laughs shrilly.

'Don't need them any more.' Her left hand dismisses the plastic bags. 'Every day you gather things that you might need in the evening or at night. Newspapers to lie on, wood to make a fire. The next day you simply start all over again. There's enough rubbish.'

We leave the terrace of half-built houses. I walk on her left.

'Single return,' I say. I'm trying to tell her that I should go back where I come from, but don't know where that is. I have no papers with me. Nothing. I must have lost everything at once, like in an earthquake.

She gives me her arm in a comradely gesture. I can feel it a bit.

'First a bite to eat,' says her voice. 'Then we'll see what the day brings.'

We cross an area of waste ground. A patch of mist sways gently over the surface of some ditches in the first warmth of the sun. Here and there scrubby bushes seem to have attracted rubbish like magnets; bits of grey plastic, empty, dented milk cartons, the bright yellow handlebars of a child's scooter.

'Let's have some more music, Kees,' I hear her say. She taps the side of the radio as it slides to and fro across my chest. I turn the dial until I hear music. A Strauss waltz.

She moves in front of me, grabs my waist and tries to waltz with me.

'Come on, let's dance, Kees!'

But I don't dare, frightened of falling into a vortex in which I might lose the rest of my body. I struggle free with one hand. Toos seems offended. She rubs her hands together and then stuffs them deep into the pockets of her greatcoat. She looks at the ground without saying anything.

'Excusing,' I say. 'I'm still living too faintly for that. It was not my intention to cause you affront.'

'It was just a bit of fun, mate. Nothing else.'

Strange that she accepts my fractured language without comment. She doesn't seem to find it odd. But perhaps she isn't listening. In any case she doesn't understand that every sentence I utter is a defeat for me compared to what I'm thinking. Shameful. I'd like to try again, but I'm frightened of getting further and further away from where I started. It's language that's leading me, not me leading the words as I should. Once I was able to speak like everyone else, wasn't I?

Sparrows flutter over the short grass on the patch of ground. Beyond it I can see a few cars moving. There must be a road there. I watch the cars go and then, turning with them, see where they are driving to. Several tower blocks rise up out of the landscape. There are a few cars here and there in the car parks in front of them. The sun is shining on the bottom rows of windows, gilding the tinted glass.

'Yes,' says Toos. 'That's where we're going. I used to work there, in those offices. In the evenings after five I had to empty the waste-paper baskets and clean the toilets. I can't understand how people can work there. You can't open anything. Until I realized you don't really

35

need money at all. If you know your way around you can get everything for free. Food, clothes, everything.'

'An eating establishment would be welcome,' I agree.

'Don't get your hopes up too high,' says Toos. 'But we'll see what's on the menu today. You've no idea the kind of things that get thrown away. One-day-old bread. As if it was poisoned. They chuck whole packs out with the rubbish. You can eat all you want, and what you can't finish you can feed to the gulls.'

We're now walking along a two-lane road. Just before the tower blocks another road meets ours. There are traffic signs and traffic lights. The signs are round or triangular and have symbols painted on them to which I can no longer react. They do seem familiar, though. Circles, crosses, arrows and figures. They refer to situations I once knew, I'm sure. They are symbols for controlling traffic, but I no longer have any part in it.

The building we are walking towards rests on two (of course actually on four) concrete piles. We look through the glass walls on the ground floor into a spacious marble-lined hall. Right in the middle, as though on an island, a man sits at a counter poking his ear with a ballpoint pen. Right in the middle, and a moment later the edge of an image which is abruptly cut off.

'This is Johnson Brothers,' says Toos. 'Don't ask me what they do, but they have a big canteen at the back.'

We walk through the gallery. My left hip has again ceased to exist, but my fingers and toes go on joining in with the rest of me. I can deduce from their tingling that the left side is there somewhere. It follows the rest of me meekly, obviously involuntarily, but unfeeling. At the back of the tower block we come to a lawn. A fountain spouts from a pond. On the other side there is an identical tower block full of gleaming windows. Two men in dazzling white shirts talking to each other go in through glass doors that automatically slide open for them. Toos points to a container on wheels, against the windowless back wall.

'There's the restaurant!'

Judging by her tone she's joking, but her remark still worries me. I mean, if she starts making mistakes too, and gives things the wrong name, where will it end?

She stops next to the container. With a couple of deft movements she takes off the cumbersome greatcoat and puts it over my arm. I stand there like a coatstand while she clambers up the container and grabs the top. Half hanging over the bin with her black dress hitched up above her thighs, she rummages around inside. 'Catch!' she shouts, but my body is already carrying her coat. With half a body you can do only half a job. A paper bag comes flying out in my direction. She lowers herself, jumps to the ground and runs to the bag.

'Here,' she says, 'see what I mean?' She unfolds the bag. 'Almost a whole white loaf.'

When I see the bread I immediately feel hungry. I take two slices from the bag and bite into them. The coat slides off my arm on to the ground.

Toos bends down and picks it up. 'Fine gentleman you are.' She holds the coat up to me. I understand what she means. I ought to help her into her coat. I'd like to, but it's beyond my powers. I need all my concentration to steer the bread in via the right side of my mouth.

'Excuses,' I say when my mouth is empty. 'Not all communication is equally efficient yet. Fifty per cent undercapacity. Perhaps later again.'

But she has the coat on once more. We walk past the bottom of the tower blocks, chewing as we go, cross a couple of car parks where more and more cars are now gathering. I'm not clear whether there is any point to her walking.

So I enquire, 'Where is the movement going to?'

'Wherever our feet take us,' she says with her mouth full. So there's no point. It doesn't matter. I wouldn't know where to go anyway. If you don't know where you've come from any more, you don't know where you have to go.

The crusts of the bread are as tough as elastic. When I pull them away from the bread with my teeth and throw them on the ground, Toos immediately picks them up.

'We don't throw anything away here,' she says, stuffing the crusts into a pocket of her green greatcoat.

As we walk along I turn the radio back on. Toos doesn't react to the music. Scarlatti. I try to turn the radio up, but even with the volume knob at maximum the music still sounds faint.

Scarlatti. Why am I so sure? Music from my previous life? I listen intently. My body reacts enthusiastically too, but in a more muted way than yesterday. It bobs lightly up and down, tries to fill the area between my toes and fingertips, but abandons the attempt a little way below the hip, as though the nerve pathways there first falter and then fade away.

My body? That's no longer how I experience it. The body accommodates me, but may partly or completely abandon or forget me at any moment. It hasn't affected my thinking, but has blocked my ability to speak the words I'm thinking, so that I'm constantly forced to find escape routes, sidetracks, which in turn bring me to other sidetracks, further and further away from the original statement with its simple meaning. As long as I don't speak I feel fairly normal. That's why I no longer try

38

to speak. My body. The moment I try to speak I feel imprisoned by it. In the past it said nothing. Now all it does is contradict me.

'Can we have that sloppy stuff off?'

I obey. Without plastic bags Toos looks quite normal. An actress astray on a building site. Or someone left behind by a circus.

'There's going to be a whole new industrial estate here,' says Toos as she points to two big signs on posts in the middle of the sandy area. There are letters painted on them.

'A year ago there were still farmhouses here,' she says. 'I often used to visit them. When the men were out in the fields you could sometimes drop in for a cup of coffee and a slice of bread. But then everything was compulsorily purchased. God knows what happened to the people. Everything's buried under the sand. Soon a few hundred people will be sitting up there gawping at their screen things.'

Her lace-up boots sink deep into the sand. The heels leave square depressions in it. My shoes are quite loose-fitting, sand gets in between my toes, but I don't mind because it's the first time my toes have all touched something at the same time again. There's obviously reconstruction work going on somewhere inside.

'Did you hear what I said?'

'Moving forward. Progression. Everything under the ground. I heard you very well.'

'You spout like a computer. But anyway, I believed in it too, progress. You got into debt. Just had to have what your neighbours had. Till Thomas dropped dead at work one day. His heart. At first I was at my wits' end. That's how the wandering really started. Anything rather than stay at home. I went further and further, right out of town. Look!'

She points to a distant point I can't reach. I turn a hundred-and-eighty degrees. A tight-knit flock of gulls hovers over a dull green inner dike. We can easily hear their cries from here.

'The rubbish tip,' she says.

'The waste heap?'

'Exactly. We're going to take a look.'

I stare at her in puzzlement.

'A gold mine,' she assures me, with a determined nod of her flower-covered head.

We leave the sandy ground and descend to a narrow strip of grass stretching down to the dike. There are cowpats everywhere, but no sign of any cows. A few clouds drag slow-moving black shadows across the short grass which here and there is already yellowing. I turn right round slowly, look at one of those shadows floating towards us. For a moment I'm in its chill clutches. Then I'm returned to the sun.

The cries of the gulls are even clearer now. Toos has started climbing up the inner dike. I have fallen a little behind, but she pays no attention. When she reaches the top she takes the paper bag with what's left of the bread out of her long coat. She tosses a piece of bread into the air and almost immediately the flapping cloud of gulls is above her. With their necks bent the birds dive for the bread she has thrown up.

On all fours I start climbing up the inner dike as well. My nostrils delight in the pungent smell of grass. I sink to the ground for a moment, laying my head in the cool grass. I start to feel something like the contour of my face, but perhaps that's imagination, just the memory of how it once felt, that face of mine. Above me the gulls mill around shrieking. I crawl upwards. The radio hits me painfully on the chin a few times.

When I reach the top, Toos is standing triumphantly among the birds on the dike. Her thick curly hair flies around her turning head as she crumbles the bread in her hands and throws it up. When she sees me her mouth breaks into a grin.

'I keep them round me like this,' she cries above the noise of the birds.

Like a lion tamer, she seems to be training the birds as they come sailing out of the sky from all directions. I recognize that feeling and smile. I once fed birds too, somewhere long ago; in a park perhaps? Ducks which came sprinting towards me over the water with their wings flapping. My little hand tried to throw the squares of bread as far away as possible, because I was frightened of them.

There are sparrows fluttering in among the gulls, but they have little chance. Only when a gull drops a piece of bread in the air and by some miracle it escapes the advancing beaks of the birds flying below is there occasionally something left for the chirping sparrows on the ground.

After throwing the last pieces of bread in the air, Toos rubs her hands together for some time. The gulls continue to circle above her for a little while, but then slowly head off in all directions. I watch them go and make out three enormous mounds of waste down below. And now I can also smell the heavy stale smell of slowly rotting rubbish. Here and there clouds of smoke curl out of the mounds.

'The gold mine,' cries Toos and begins climbing down the dike.

'*King Solomon's Mines*,' I shout back, amazed at how I'd

hit on that. Somehow I know for certain that it's the title of a book. I try to turn my half body into the best possible position before starting the steep descent.

The ribbed tyre tracks of trucks are visible in wide brown cinder paths between the mounds. There is no one else on the refuse tip. Now and then a little cloud of sickly sweet stench pops out of the side of one of the mounds. My body protests, tries to turn away from the stench, but I don't dare lose sight of Toos. She is walking around purposefully, as though she comes here often. I examine the mounds a little more carefully. Much of the rubbish has lost its original shape. Here and there the coloured label of a tin emerges from the shapeless heap. A fork sticks out of a muddy brown substance and suggests a relationship which suddenly turns my stomach. Parts of the heap are scorched black. A blue plastic crate has great bubbles on it, like blisters.

I follow Toos to the furthermost mound. This is different from the other two. It is lower and made of less perishable material. What the public health department calls 'bulky items'. Bedsprings, a dresser with gaping holes where there were once panes of glass, slats of wood covered with bent protruding nails, chairs without backs, lop-sided refrigerators with white doors opened wide, lots of plastic objects in garish colours, an indoor clothes dryer with pegs still attached to it, shreds of clothing, a cardboard box full of plastic beach shoes. Everything is in a state of unstable equilibrium now being disturbed by Toos as she starts nimbly scaling the mound. What is she looking for? Now and then something tumbles down under her weight. A round steel ball detaches itself, rolls across a door half sticking out of the heap and then falls to the ground with a thud, like the successful climax to a music-hall turn.

'Cautious,' I shout. 'Cheerful.' Both wrong, but she can't hear me anyway. She has now clambered to the very top of the heap and, leaning forward with her feet wide apart, is rummaging in a pile of planks. She has taken her hat off and put it down next to her. She has got hold of something heavy, I can see that from the repeated straining of her bent back to lift it up. Now she has got the object and turns round unsteadily on the unreliable surface.

In her hand she is holding a sewing machine, gleaming black and attached to a shiny, varnished wooden base. She looks around, working out the best route down the mound with the thing. Bending slightly at the knees she slides down a foot at a time.

'A Singer!' she shouts to me triumphantly. 'A real Singer!'

'You can sew now,' I cry enthusiastically.

'We can sow wild oats, if you like,' she says with a leer as she takes the last breathless, diagonal, half-sliding steps down. She lowers the sewing machine carefully to the ground in front of her. She stands up and puts her hands on her waist to straighten her back. 'Christ, what a weight!'

She looks down approvingly at the sewing machine.

'Antique,' she says. 'A real Singer. They fetch a fortune nowadays.'

'Does it still operate satisfactorily?' I ask. Whoever is regulating my speech expresses himself more formally than I would like. But perhaps formality is just unnecessary long-windedness.

'Doesn't matter,' says Toos, still out of breath from her climb. 'As long as it's antique. People like having old things in the house. First they chuck everything out and

43

then they want it back again. I'm going to flog this one straight away.'

She takes a couple of steps back and surveys me thoughtfully. Then she briskly extends her hand. 'I'm leaving you, Kees,' she says. 'I want to get to town before the shops close.'

She bends down and lifts the sewing machine, with a supreme effort, hoisting it on to her left shoulder.

'Best of luck, Kees.'

She turns round and starts walking away from me.

'Doos,' I cry. 'Don't go. Your had! Your had!'

But Toos doesn't turn round again. She disappears hatless across the brown cinders behind the rubbish heaps. I turn quickly on my axis a few times. As the tears well up in my eyes it seems as though her presence in my head is suppressed once she's out of my sight. A chair sticks its seat invitingly out of the mound. I pull it out and sit down on it. The radio rests against my chest.

It's strange, but life refuses to make a real impression on me, as though it's not really mine. Toos, as a figure of flesh and blood, seems never really to have got through to me, although I saw her a moment ago walking in her black lace-up boots along the cinder path and disappearing behind a rubbish heap for ever with the sewing machine on her shoulder.

I see everything but I no longer experience what happens as something that affects me personally. It just happens to me. And the memory of what has happened is colourless and detached. 'I'm leaving you, Kees.' Now it sounds like a line from a play. She was right when she stood in front of me naked. 'You're gawping as if you're in a museum.' Her breasts with the brown freckles around the slightly pimply nipples, the joyous tuft of

44

pubic hair between her skinny thighs. Signals which no longer reached my blunted senses. Obviously other people's bodies are as unreal to me as my own.

Seated on the old chair with its bulging reddish-brown seat I look around me. Three seagulls glide overhead, riding the wind. I'm already breathing in the heavy smell of decay without revulsion. I recognize that smell from a flat waste barge, where I and my playmates used to hunt for sanitary towels. Filled with disgust and excitement, we studied the brown stains which had soaked deep into the absorbent layer of the towel. Women bled, once a month, although we had never seen that. Finally we would pelt each other with the towels we had found until an inspector from the public health department or an elderly woman passing by on a bike chased us off the barge.

Again my eyes fill with tears. I never used to cry, and now tears seem to seize every opportunity. I have to cry because this memory is so sharp and clear and vivid and my surroundings so dull and toneless. I emerged from a rich, scented world full of sounds and happenings. And now? What's happened to that world?

Now I can imagine what it's like to be colour-blind. There are colours hidden behind all those various shades of grey, colours which have become inaccessible for ever. Everything you see becomes permeated with the melancholy of an irrevocable loss. There has been an intervention from inside. The question is whether it is irreversible or whether there is a way back, a chance for recovery.

My eyes scour the dump for worn-out household effects. The quantity of bedsprings is striking, as though a large part of the population regularly decides to buy a new bed (or to stop sleeping). The hose of a vacuum cleaner in this environment of complete degradation and decay has a slightly comic effect. It makes me think of the rubbish bag in its plastic interior, perhaps still filled with the dust of the house where it gave up the ghost.

Detached spherical table legs, a fire grate, red with rust, a washbasin with a triangular hole in the round porcelain bowl, a dismantled children's game of Electro. I get up.

Once they were intact, formed part of a room, a room like the one I must have owned once. A collection of objects which you arranged around you in an order of their own so as to keep the chaos outside at bay. I take hold of the red and blue wires in the Electro game. At the end of the wires there should be the sorts of plugs which fit into the round holes in the cardboard box. I see a little boy with blond hair putting the plugs into the holes and beaming when the lamp in the middle of the box glows red. Where does the image come from? Is that me as I used to be, or is it a child of mine? It must be the second, the game didn't exist when I was a boy. But I can't remember having children, or a wife. It's possible. Perhaps it's just something I read about somewhere. I turn away from the game, allow it to disappear into the part of my field of vision where everything becomes invisible as if by magic.

I walk slowly round the mound of household rubbish. I don't dare climb it with my only half-functioning body. Then my eye is caught by an object that I don't immediately recognize. Panic seizes me because I know I ought to recognize it. I do know, but the knowledge is concealed, out of reach. I put out my hand hesitantly, stroke the white-painted iron tube which ends in a milky white bowl. At the bottom of the tube there is a round shiny steel base from which a lead comes out ending in a plug.

46

My fingers feel the inside of the bowl and pull it towards me out of the heap. Then they disappear into a round brass opening. I can feel the thread on the inside. All the details of the object accumulate in me, like the parts of a sentence. Only when my fingers reach the bottom of the opening and strike a kind of small catch does my body yield up the name. Lamp. The round opening is called the fitting. You screw a bulb into it, stick the plug into the point and there is light. I pull the lamp right out, and, turning round, make my way back towards the chair and put the lamp next to it. I sit down, holding the lamp by the tube like a wand. Strange. Already I can't imagine that just now I had no idea of its name or what it was for. It might have been anything. You can't live like that. The fingers of my right hand stroke the smooth tube. Lamp.

It's not so much that there are blank areas in my knowledge, as I thought before when at first I had a problem recognizing the transistor. No, my knowledge isn't full of gaps, it's just stored differently, filed according to a system I scarcely know yet. Something has reprogrammed me, and as a result I can no longer retrieve information that I know I have somewhere. Sometimes music comes to my aid, sometimes my sense of touch. Only language refuses to obey me. Letters no longer mean anything (that girl's sweater in the snack bar was covered with illegible messages) and there is no longer the obvious hatch between thinking and speaking that was always there in the past.

Nevertheless I must use systematic experiments to find out exactly where and how the connections got disrupted. Once I've cracked that programme I may be able to adapt my language to the new code. But what if the code is simply inaccessible to my battered consciousness? Mustn't think about it. We must get on.

Some objects sticking out of the grey heap have lost so many of their components that it's impossible to deduce their previous function. An iron sheet, painted green, with holes of various sizes and shapes punched in it (small and large circles, punched squares at either end) was once the base of something, but because the rest of it is missing it has become unnameable, in the same way that everything here is on its way to becoming unrecognizable. Or is it simply me after all and ought I to know the purpose that this sheet with holes in it once served? Mustn't think about it.

Suddenly I feel a stab in my left hip. Pain which suddenly revives my hope that my body is still seeking its own image. As though, just like me, it had lost some of its memories and was now trying to trace them.

I turn on the radio and search for a music station. I recognize a drawing-room piece for violin and piano from the last century. It is so faint that it can't get right through to the left side, however close I hold the radio to my ear. Though the whole of my left leg does start tingling, as if outlining its contours on a blank map, it refuses to move independently, whatever command I send with my thoughts. I search for another station which may have a stronger signal. But all the stations are just as faint. The batteries must be running down.

With the by now almost inaudible radio hanging from my neck I walk slowly round the mound. The music is still just loud enough to give me back the left side of my field of vision, so that I can see larger portions of the rubbish tip at the same time. I hunt for discarded objects which may contain batteries with a little energy left in them. People often throw broken equipment away with batteries and all, even if they've only just put them in. But try as I may, I can't find any now. I hear the radio slowly fading, first making just a soft hissing sound and finally falling completely silent. My first concern is to find new batteries. And something to eat.

I walk back to the chair, turn off the radio and open the flap at the back. I pull out two oblong batteries from the niche and put them in my pocket. Then I hang the radio back round my neck. I'd rather keep it in my hand, but I'm frightened it will end up in the missing part of the world so I won't be able to find it again.

The sun has moved round, and is now shining from behind me. I get up. I glance at the standard lamp and the chair in the middle of the path. They look like the elements of an interior, a parody of earlier surroundings. An image of a conservatory of climbing plants and wicker furniture looms up that I can't immediately place. Imaginary pictures and real memories may be jumbled up perhaps. That possibility doesn't exactly cheer me up. Most of all I need unambiguous facts. But how can I tell the difference between a real memory and something that I've read or am simply imagining? Has that ability to distinguish been lost or is it hiding elsewhere? I feel that my body is bigger than it was, has expanded into infinity and this makes me feel so giddy that I can't help closing my eyes when I think of it. I always had a body, but only now am I learning its true, vast nature.

Two

I hear a motor vehicle approaching, its engine heavier than a car's but lighter than a lorry's. I quickly turn round a number of times, but can't see anything coming my way. Without the help of the radio I can only go right, where screaming gulls rise from the piles of rubbish. I crouch down behind a wheel-less delivery bike which has fallen on its side. I hear doors slamming, a man's voice, then another answering. I get up cautiously and peer over the wooden edge of the basket. I'm looking at the side of a pick-up truck, sprayed a shabby mustard colour. There are thin streaks of mud running above the black mudguards. A man with a bristly black moustache is unloading something. The other man, younger than the one in the back, takes hold of it. When he turns round in his moss-green sweater and jeans, I can see that he is holding car number plates. He takes the number plates in the direction of the mound of bulky rubbish, and then I see him stop by the chair and the lamp for a moment, kick them over and start climbing nimbly upwards. Now and then he pauses, keeping his balance, and pushes a number plate in among the rubbish. He surveys his work, bending slightly backwards. The plates mustn't be visible. The men's profession is obvious. The man with the number plates climbs higher and higher between refrigerators, kitchen tables, dilapidated sofas and bedsprings. When he reaches the top of the heap and all the number plates have disappeared into the pile, he bends down. He picks something up, puts it on his head and dances round clumsily, finally throwing the flowered hat high into the air.

Seeing the hat acts like a magnet on my nervous system. I jump up, bumping into the delivery bike, which falls over tantalizingly slowly. 'Had,' I shout, 'Doos! Had!'

The dark-haired man with the moustache reaches me in two bounds. He grabs hold of me roughly. The transistor is pressed painfully against my breastbone. He keeps a firm hold of me while the young man takes long, springy strides down the mound of rubbish.

'What were you doing there, grandad?' asks the young man, in a friendlier voice than I'd expected. The dark man shakes me to hasten my answer. I realize that the connection between my left hip, knee, tibia and foot has been suddenly restored. Because of fear? I'm so confused that I don't answer.

'Let him go,' orders the young man. His hands are gleaming with oil. When the man with the moustache lets go of me I feel the co-ordination with my left side ebbing away. I turn involuntarily to the right.

The dark man drags me back close to his face again. 'No running off, right?'

'Faithful,' I stammer. 'In good faith, I mean!'

The young man steps forward. He's now standing next to his colleague. Or are they brothers? They have the same nose coming straight out of their foreheads.

'What did you see?'

The dark man is beginning to get impatient. His hands disappear into the pockets of his corduroy trousers.

'You relinquished number plates,' I say.

'Hey, do you always talk like that?' says the young one, with a chilly, fleeting smile.

'I don't trust him,' says the dark man. 'He's playing dumb.' He snorts deeply like an animal, his moustache turns down lop-sidedly.

'I got into linguistic confusion. All explanation is arduous.'

Again my power of speech, the anonymous centre which governs it at present, opts for a roundabout, far too formal version of what I mean.

'He's either a professor or he's stupid. One of the two,' the young one concludes.

'I don't trust him,' repeats the moustache.

'Then we'll take him with us for interrogation,' sniggers the young one, winking. The other man seems to find this a good idea. He grabs me and pushes me in the direction of the back of the truck. 'Off you go,' he says. 'Get in.'

By the tailgate, which is hanging down, he suddenly lifts me up with both arms. I struggle in the air. With both legs! Then I land with a crash against the back wall of the driver's cab, where the young chap is starting the engine.

The man with the moustache squats opposite me. He holds on to the side walls of the truck with arms outstretched.

'Put that radio on.' It sounds like an order.

'The current's dead,' I say, putting my hand protectively on the aluminium case on my chest.

'You mean the batteries are flat,' he says.

I nod.

'Well, say so then,' he replies in an accent that seems vaguely familiar. The man is a complete stranger to me, but I know the dialect he's speaking.

I have no idea how long I've been living here in the car cemetery. Karel and Cor – they *are* brothers – have put me up in a wheel-less caravan at the back of the site. There is a bed and some yellowy light is provided by an oil lamp hanging from the ceiling. They themselves live in a permanently parked trailer close to the entrance to the site, closed off from the surrounding fields by an improvised fence. During the day they are usually out and about in their truck. Then I walk around the site with their little keeshond, Sara. Sometimes I chase a couple of boys messing around on the site back over the fence, shouting wildly. That gives me a pleasant feeling, a feeling of returning power.

I have noticed that my memory is working a little better. Not so long ago events seemed to flow through me without my being able to retain very much. Now one or two things stick again, although I'm not completely sure of the precise order in which they have happened. But at least something of the sense of living in time, in the same time to which Karel and Cor belong, has returned. Cor, the youngest, has given me a watch. I remember the connection between the movements of the sun and the hands on the watch. But I didn't admit to him that I can no longer tell the time. Nevertheless those moving hands give my day content, like the sequence of chapter numbers in a novel. (Where did I get this comparison from? It seems to mean more to me than an example chosen at random.)

I still don't have complete control over the left side of my field of vision. Things regularly tumble out of it, but their partial or complete absence no longer causes the wild panic it did at first. I know that they're there, and they will stay there, that the world doesn't move.

But I did have a terrible fright one day when Karel threw me a paper, and ordered me to read it aloud. Not only could I no longer read the paper (as I had more or less expected), but the beginning of every sentence that I had read now seemed to have vanished! And if I scanned further along the lines, the rest of the sentence also disappeared, as if somewhere there on the left a vacuum cleaner was sucking up all the words and all the letters.

The strange thing was that they appeared relieved when I shook my head sadly, pushed the paper away and tried to explain to them that I could no longer read. That announcement cheered them up. Perhaps their cheerfulness was also the result of drink; they were downing pints from early morning onwards.

Apart from that they dealt with my speech problems in a fairly matter-of-fact way. Cor particularly was bright enough to guess the correct meanings behind all those wrongly placed sentences of mine. Sometimes he put me back on the right track halfway through a fragmented sentence. For example, he knew immediately that by 'nut spread' I meant 'peanut butter'. Karel was amazed. For him I was simply disturbed. Perhaps Cor thought the same, but in some way he saw what was going on, saw that there was a pattern in the disturbance, a kind of logic, and that I wasn't simply saying whatever came into my head.

Karel is a taciturn, surly man. To begin with when they brought me with them to this place he was very suspicious. He couldn't be made to understand that I simply couldn't go to the police because they wouldn't be able to understand me. That was why Karel locked me up at first when they went out. Then one evening in the trailer Cor had shown that I couldn't betray Karel. He pretended to be a detective and interrogated me. Now that he was no longer helping me to put my thoughts into words, I lost the thread within a few seconds. 'You see,' he had said to Karel after a while. 'He may know, but in any case he can't say.' After that Karel left the gate open when they went out.

That's precisely what makes me so desperate. I understand everything that's said, but taking part in the conversation myself is more or less impossible. Mostly I resort to simple text, sentences of about four words. That's why I prefer playing cards with them, four-card brag or pontoon. Still, I mustn't lose heart. I used to be in control of my language, now my body is. Yet sometimes there are chinks which allow a connection to be made without interference. That means it's still possible.

The left side of my body now seems to have woken up for good. The tingling in my fingertips and toes has disappeared, my left hand and foot are now simply present the whole time, silently and self-evidently. The hip has also become sensitive. Now the thigh tingles as far as the kneecap. But below that the body (or its reflection) abandons me again, there's a blind spot. Or actually not even that. That is where formlessness begins, the space in the world, separate from the things which give it sense, substance. Once – in an earlier, different life I'm inclined to think – I never experienced that space in that way. Perhaps it didn't exist or in some way I was resistant to it, like a virus. Now I experience it as a force which is constantly present, out to eliminate me, disrupt my thinking and cancel out my body. At such moments I cringe and hide my face in my hands, or hurt myself, in the hope that the pain will drive out the panic. After a while I can feel the fear subsiding, the pressure on my body lessening and my thinking returning to well-defined channels. But what remains is the memory of a kind of murderous attack from which I escaped by the skin of my teeth. But what is attacking me: my body or the space beyond it?

Still, it's obvious that processes are going on inside me that are trying to restore the old connections, to reconstruct the inner space, which enables me to assess the space outside more and more easily and perhaps even to control it again.

During the day I walk around the car cemetery with Sara. At first I had scarcely any notion of its size. Sometimes it seemed endless, and then at other times to my astonishment I immediately bumped into the lop-sided gate beyond which lay the fields and the ditches.

Sometimes I stand at the gate for ages looking out at the cropped grass trembling in the wind, at the grazing cows and sheep or at the silhouette of a farmer on a tractor. Somehow it revives a memory for me. I'm sure this landscape is connected in some way with my earlier life. Two ducks paddling round in a ditch between two fields quack, and suddenly an image glides forward, so clear and abrupt that it makes me flinch.

I was sitting in the wooden privy at the bottom of Uncle Daan's garden. The round lid lay next to me on the throne, as Uncle Daan called the wooden box with the round hole in the middle. The privy had been built over a ditch. Before I climbed on to the throne I always looked into the hole first. Once two ducks suddenly appeared beneath and quacked loudly, their wide-open beaks raised aloft. I was so frightened that suddenly I lost all urge to use the lavatory.

Uncle Daan was the fattest man in our family. In the semi-circular built-in ovens he baked not only bread, but also enormous quantities of biscuits, smelling of traditional spices, which he pulled out of the oven on large black baking trays with his huge dinner-plate hands coloured dull white with flour. I was woken at five in the morning by Uncle Daan. I was allowed to help him stoke up the oven, with embers still glowing from the previous day, into which sacks of rustling coal disappeared. Standing at the gate, I sniff the gassy smell of the coal, feel my mouth water when I think of the spiced biscuits, hard and still warm, which he pushed in my direction.

I've never thought of Uncle Daan and the bakery since. He's long dead and the bakery was sold to someone who started up a bicycle shop. But he still lives in me, fat and smelling of bread and spiced biscuits with his trembling double chins and his formidable paunch over which his white apron is stretched taut.

Of course I have childhood memories, like everyone else, but in my new situation they present themselves with the total clarity of a moment in the present. As if there is no essential difference and all the moments of your life are always there, down to the last detail. There, but not always retrievable, sometimes hiding in the folds of an inhibiting present. Because where exactly was that bakery? What was the name of that village?

I can see the street in front of me. There were several shops, a dairy with a large glass bowl full of white and brown eggs in the window, a butcher's with a classroom diagram of a large cow on the tiled back wall. The cow was divided into sections by straight black lines within which the name of the relevant joint of meat was printed.

57

I must have absorbed this as a child while shopping, and now it all comes up again, as though I am that child again and am standing there with my mother's shopping list clutched in my hand. No, Uncle Daan lived in another village. But what village was this then?

A line of elms sways on the horizon. Windbreaks. Crows flapping around seem to be annoyed by the strong wind which ruffles their feathers. They croak loudly and rebelliously.

The little keeshond has crawled into an Opel with no doors. I sit down at the steering wheel next to the dog. The word windbreak is still echoing in my head. That word too is connected with the past, with my childhood, with a father who cycled along a dike, one hand on his hat against the wind, to warn the midwife that a child was on the way.

The keeshond next to me pants in short bursts, its thin, pink, trembling tongue hanging out of its mouth.

I look through the dirty windscreen at the half-overlapping cars in the breaker's yard.

I still had great difficulty finding my way around because I could only see one part of the site and couldn't join the separate parts into a unity in my head. So as to get my bearings better I had started putting shiny hub caps down in certain places which I numbered with black paint (I remembered numbers in their correct sequence perfectly. It was just that I could no longer apply the functions to them that I had once learned at school, with which you could combine them, make them move).

One evening I tried to make a kind of map of the site. Cor had to help me because the left-hand side of the map

58

kept disappearing and I had to turn right round several times to imprint that part in my memory. I felt like an inventor in search of an invention, excited at the idea, but completely aimless, without any kind of plan. That evening I discovered neither of them could write. (I still could, although oddly enough I couldn't read what I had written myself.) That surprised me. The map was no more than a rough oblong with a wide circle of numbers drawn inside it, in clockwise order. I kept counting again and again, beginning at one. Finally I had a map in my hands which I couldn't read. Nevertheless it helped me to feel I was gaining more of a grip on my surroundings.

Cor understood, he said. When he had to go to a place where he had never been before, he also made signs in the road so as to be able to find the way back; a private map which he superimposed on the existing map of those who could read.

With me it was different. I could write, but afterwards couldn't read what I had written. As soon as I consigned the letters to paper their meaning vanished from my head. As though writing erased my thoughts. That's why I stopped immediately, however fascinated Karel was when he looked on. He didn't believe that I couldn't read what I myself had just written, but Cor understood – or he pretended to.

Cor and I often spent the evenings alone in the trailer. Karel was out a couple of times a week. On a job, as he called it, or seeing a woman whose name was never mentioned. On those evenings Cor cooked on the three-burner gas stove. Usually he opened a tin, of which the brothers seemed to have an inexhaustible supply. Brown beans were a particular favourite.

Cor was a nervous, talkative lad, who suffered visibly

under the regime of his surly brother. He wanted to quit, return to society, as he called it, but his brother wouldn't let him go. Moreover, Karel said, who wants someone who's been inside? You'll never get any work out there. Karel talked about society as though it was somewhere abroad. The brothers never spoke about the past. It was as though they had always lived in that car cemetery, far from the inhabited world.

When Cor was alone with me he dared to speak freely. He could get quite carried away talking about his plans. One day he'd go to school and learn to read, and the world would be his oyster. 'It's ridiculous really,' he said. 'You learn to talk by yourself, but you have to learn to write.'

One evening, with a very roundabout use of words which came thronging from all sides, I tried to explain my situation to him. It's as if – I said, more or less – I first have to translate everything from another language before I can start to speak. Sometimes I hit upon a word that's close to what I want to say but is just wide of the mark. You have no idea how terrible that is. As though you've suddenly become too stupid for words.

With the help of the map the jumble of cars and piles of separate parts, distributed by type over the site, seemed to be interconnected again. Gradually the area took on an order for me, so that with scarcely any effort I could find parts for Karel, which he then loaded into the van in the mornings to take them off somewhere to sell. After a while – I'm still not sure exactly how long – I left the map in the caravan. The area was now in my head. Although I still regularly lost sight of the left side, the absent portion of the world was almost immediately filled with a mental perception of it, based on, or at least created with the help of the map, which I had pinned to one of the walls of the caravan.

When Cor and Karel sometimes go off together in the evenings, like now, I sit here with Sara in the trailer listening to the radio into which Cor has put new batteries for me. I have the impression that music – particularly classical music – has a salutary effect on the left-hand side of my body. How far it has a permanent effect I shall have to wait and see. At least while the music is on the beginning of a sentence no longer disappears from sight when I look at the newspaper in front of me. My hands perform co-ordinated actions for as long as the music lasts. If it suddenly stops, my hands go on repeating their last movements for minutes, as though the music has put a spell on them. Similarly I can get stuck on one word. The word windbreak for example. It's a word I can pronounce without any problem and which appears able to join together all kinds of actions, although Cor and Karel do not understand why I am constantly mumbling 'windbreak' while I sit spooning my soup.

The hands of the illuminated watch on my wrist overlap each other precisely at the top of the dial. Sara is lying asleep on the other seat with her head on her front paws.

'There's no place like home.'

I've discovered that virtually all proverbs come out intact. Sometimes I mumble whole series of them in bed, for the sheer pleasure of connected speech, no longer being just off the mark, although the senseless stringing together of sayings wouldn't have meant much to anyone else.

I get up and turn the oil lamp on the ceiling down low. Sara momentarily lifts her pointed head; when she sees

61

me pull back the bed covers she lets her head sink back on to her front paws and closes her eyes.

Waking with a start for a moment I don't know where I am for a moment; in my dream, in reality or somewhere else (as used to happen to me in the past when I was a child, a short period of bewilderment from which I emerged gasping for breath). In the subdued pool of light from the oil lamp, which has been turned up high, I can see Cor with Sara in his arms. Karel is standing in the doorway of the caravan and motions me to get out of bed.

'We need you for a job,' says Cor, stroking the little dog's muzzle.

'At once?' I ask and tap the dial of my watch. 'At this point in time?'

'Get dressed,' he says.

I hang the transistor round my neck and search for a station. Getting dressed goes with scarcely a hitch; so long as there is music. A Dutch female voice sings about loneliness and holidays.

'Christ,' growls Karel, leaning in the doorway. 'Do you have to, at this hour?'

'Let him be,' said Cor and hands him the little dog. 'Here, you lock Sara up.'

I feel a lot more at ease alone with Cor. Squatting down, he helps me tie the shoelaces which he took out of an old pair of shoes of his when I arrived here. Now I can turn the music off.

'During this,' I began. 'No hand in front of face. How are you going to bring it off?'

'We know where we have to go,' says Cor and gets up.

'Do unto others.' I point to the tied shoelaces. 'What actions have to be accomplished?'

Cor pushes me gently but firmly ahead of him towards the outside steps of the caravan.

'Acting as lookout,' he says. 'Listening in case anyone comes. That's all. Do you understand?'

I nod. Cor holds me by one arm. It isn't really necessary, it's a clear night. A lorry's raised bonnet casts a sharp shadow which we have to pass through (shadows have substance for me, for Cor they obviously don't).

Karel is already outside by the gate next to the truck. Each headlight casts a long beam on to a bumpy road, where the worst potholes have been filled with rubble. I look along the beams of the headlights and see gnats and small insects dancing to the edge of the light, where the air starts undulating so that I mustn't look at it for too long.

'I've told him,' says Cor to Karel.

'Well? Has he understood?'

'Yes, haven't you?'

I nod. I have to sit next to Cor in the cab. Karel climbs into the back.

Not many people live hereabouts. Most farms stand unlit at the foot of the dikes. We drive down long, straight roads. The poplars on either side of the road rush past us in the light of the headlights. There is no other traffic. Far in the distance an orange flame burns. A strange sight, a separate flame suspended in the dark night. But I know there's a chimney underneath it. Fortunately the world no longer consists solely of direct observations; I can supplement what I see with what I know again, with what I remember from previous observations.

The truck's engine makes me sleepy. I nod off a few times, and wake again with a start when my chin strikes the transistor. Cor peers tensely ahead of him. I look round briefly, but can't see anything out of the cab's dark window.

Suddenly the road turns to the left. Yet Cor goes straight on. He makes no move to turn the steering wheel left. A strangled, hoarse sound rises from my throat. I try to grab his arm, pull the steering wheel to the left, but Cor pushes me away with a violent blow of the hand.

'Bastard, do you want us to have an accident, or what?'

I don't reply. I'm sure I saw the road going left and now I'm suddenly also sure that I used to drive a car.

They call it night blindness. I preferred not to drive at night because I saw all kinds of things which turned out not to be there. A kind of hallucination, said the doctor. Especially when people are overtired it can affect them. I laugh at this vivid memory that suddenly looms up, like the trees and the dark farm sheds along the roadside. Night blindness.

'Yes, you can laugh,' says Cor, 'we could have been killed. We'll be there any minute.'

He slows down, and then brakes gently at a side road. The headlights pick out a barrier across the middle of the road, a plank on two iron supports. Cor stops. I hear Karel jump out of the back. He walks to the road block, lifts up the plank so that Cor can turn into the narrow dirt road. With the engine running he waits until Karel has jumped back into the rear of the truck and bangs on the window of the cab with the flat of his hand. We move off again.

'No through road. Signs like that are always useful,' says Cor as we slowly bump down the road. Then he stops and dims the headlights. For a moment nothing can be seen out of the front windscreen. I hear Karel getting out of the back. He opens the door on Cor's side.

Once I'm out my eyes have already got used to the dark. To the right of the road, about ten yards away from us, is a small farmhouse with a haystack and a barn next to it.

'We need to be in that barn for a little while,' whispers Cor. 'You watch the top two windows. That's where they sleep. The moment you see light up there you wave this torch.'

He thrusts a torch into my hand.

I nod. I see them walking ahead of me down the road. Two brothers. You wouldn't think so from the silhouettes. One of them heavy, with the swaying gait of a tough guy, Cor next to him, frail and tense and tiptoeing along. They walk down the moonlit road and disappear behind a haystack.

Of course they're off stealing, but the how and the why of it doesn't interest me in the least. I focus on the top windows at the front of the farmhouse. The newly painted eaves under the thatched roof glow white. On the lawn in front of the house is a gnome and a wheelbarrow full of geraniums.

'Big Ears.' I see a book and a child's voice says, 'Go on reading, Daddy.' Daddy? I try to pay no attention to this voice which has suddenly popped into my head.

'Wouter,'* I say softly, and then focus all my attention back on the two square dark windows. This is the world, the real one. That voice. As though I have night blindness inside too for a moment.

In the silence around there is an occasional rustle, a rabbit or a hedgehog in the verge perhaps. A sound rumbles towards me from a distance. A dull rattling, as though somebody somewhere is driving a harvester down the road. My heart is in my mouth. Any sound

* Pronounced 'vow-ter'.

may wake the occupants of the farm. However, the windows stay dark and the noise suddenly stops again.

The wind has dropped, the grass at the roadside stands straight up as if staring, like me, at the mists of stars hanging in the night sky like streaks of icing sugar. Occasionally something sparkles brightly, and then disappears. The universe is moving away from us, the universe is expanding all the time. Someone must have once told me that. From the starry sky I look at the two windows behind which unsuspecting farmers are lying asleep. Cor and Karel make no sound. Another person might be frightened. Or find it an adventure. But I feel nothing. I stand there with the torch in my hand, looking at the night sky, and suddenly my name seems to emerge from the stardust, projects itself proudly in the sky and simply has to be read. Aloud.

'Kees Zomer!'

I look down again. I see them approaching in the distance, Cor and Karel. They are carrying something heavy between them. As they get nearer I can see that it is a car engine. They walk past me to the back of the truck without a word. Karel motions angrily with his moustache in the direction of the tailgate. I take out the pins on either side, first the right pin, that is. Then I walk quickly round the truck until I see the left-hand pin.

Then I realize that's no longer necessary. I no longer need to approach reality in clockwise circles. I can go straight to my target again.

Puffing and snorting, they raise the heavy engine and push it forward over the bottom of the back of the truck with a scraping sound. They leave the tailgate loose. As I am about to climb into the cab Karel grabs me roughly by my shoulder.

'In the back you,' he hisses. Cor clambers behind the

steering wheel again. Karel helps me into the back of the truck and then jumps in himself. He sits down next to me. The truck starts up, quietly and in first gear, with its headlights off. We stop at the road block. Karel jumps out and pushes first the plank and then the two stands into the back. Only when the farm is a good way behind us does Cor pick up speed. In a field I hear two startled plovers fleeing into the night with shrill cries.

'Kees Zomer.' I mumble my name softly.

'Who's that?' asked Karel.

'Me,' I say. 'My name has revived. Fallen from the sky just like that. Kees Zomer.' I point to the night sky.

Karel says nothing. We are now driving along a tarmacked road. The night air flows icily through my shirt over my chest. Forgot to stuff newspapers under it.

Then I feel his hands, Karel's huge strong hands, grabbing me, lifting me up and hurling me out of the back of the truck.

My feet land with a smack on the surface of the road, throwing me to one side, where I land in the grass and then roll head over heels through the verge into the ditch. Flashes of light shoot from left to right across my retina like lightning.

Three

I'm woken by a faint ticking above my head. As though a tap is dripping, more than one tap, and a shower of droplets is descending on the awning above me. I keep my eyes closed. I recognize that sound. Drops of water on a tent canvas.

Remember, lad, said Dad, if it starts to rain, don't lean against the canvas or it'll start leaking. But how could I control my body in the sleeping bag when I was asleep? Night after night – it rained constantly on our holidays – I tried to fall asleep on my back. Usually I woke having rolled against the canvas. Dark patches of damp had penetrated not only the wall of the tent but also my sleeping bag.

My hands grope for the zip. It isn't there, but there is a tent. I run my hands over my body. It's there, a single whole. And now the memory of the previous night slowly returns. Karel throwing me out of the van; tumbling, soft grass, the ditch smelling of leaves.

I open my eyes. I'm not lying in a tent, but under a sheet of plastic strung between poles, behind which I can see the blurred outline of passing clouds. When I raise myself up on my elbows I can see the sun's rays fanning out over the meadows a short distance away. It won't be long before it's dry here too.

My whole body is hurting. Cautiously I pull in my legs, first the right one, then the left, move the fingers of my right and then my left hand in front of my face, as Wouter used to when he was a baby, with surprised round watery eyes and a faint, impersonal smile on his lips. A baby playing with his fingers in a cot, on his back like me, staring in amazement at the world above his head.

Everything seems to be in working order, nothing's broken. I sit up carefully. Above me the last drops, slower and heavier than those earlier, are pattering on the plastic.

I look around, turn my head from left to right. I can scarcely imagine that there was a time, only a short while ago, when part of my body was lost, when I had no left hand or foot. Or was it all just imagination? Everything has reassembled into a familiar pattern, into what one means when one talks about one's body.

The earlier absence of my left side is now just as difficult to conceive of as toothache which has passed, those shooting, piercing pains in your jaw radiating to your temple and your neck. Suddenly it had disappeared as though it had never been. No, pain, once gone, is impossible to remember. It's something purely physical.

I sink to my knees, resting both hands on my kneecaps. The radio! What has happened to the transistor? I look around me, in wider and wider circles, timid and uncertain, as though my eyes still have to adjust to taking in so much splendour at once.

It's a kind of unkempt garden, strewn with wooden sheds, piles of old planks and heaps of stones between which clumps of buttercups flower. I can't see the transistor anywhere. I must have lost it when I fell last night. Or else someone has taken it from me. Someone?

Bending low, I emerge from beneath the plastic sheet,

straighten my back. In a reflex motion my hands grab at the source of the stabbing pains in my back.

Hidden behind some spreading alder trees, their dark leaves dusty, is a stone cottage with a flat tiled roof. The door is secured by an old-fashioned padlock. Next to the door is an old television on a pile of crates. A cinder path leads up a gentle slope from the house to a narrow lane through the meadows. A long cart made of tubing stands on the cinders on two bicycle wheels. A handcart, one like Dad used to have for collecting the milk churns from the dairy. The churns with deeply recessed lids which made a sucking noise as you twisted them off. The bubbles on the sloshing surface of the milk in the churn. My thoughts are wandering again. It's as though memories of long ago are tugging at me more and more strongly, trying to displace the recent past: the cart on bicycle wheels in front of me and an old man pulling me along a dike, beside a canal where the morning mist was dozing among the fringes of reeds. I can't remember any more. So I must have been conscious for an instant. Drifted off again after that, I expect. An old man.

Slowly I walk over to the cart, bend down to take hold of the pull bar, which immediately nestles pleasantly in my hand, and I'm almost off to the dairy again, to the long concrete loading platform with the rows of churns. I quickly let go of the pull bar and walk back to the house.

The door is locked. The old man has gone. I vaguely remember his face. A sunken mouth, cheeks red from living outdoors (like Dad's), small, deep-set blue eyes. I must have seen that in a flash when I regained consciousness, sighed perhaps, and the old man pulling the cart had looked round for a moment to see how I was.

I walk across the area, still vaguely looking for the radio, although I no longer need it as a guideline for my body which now moves forward of its own account as though it has never done any differently.

The sheds are a little larger than dog kennels. I deduce from the small round droppings everywhere in the grass that goats live in them, but there are no goats to be seen anywhere. In the middle of the site, surrounded by a fence which the old man has knocked together from all kinds of bits of timber, is a rock garden with the same improvised look as the fence. Fragments of rubble and loose stones have been laid in a careless pattern in the earthen wall. There are not only pink phloxes, but also white foxgloves. Shrivelled daffodil stalks poke up between the stones. A small bed of marigolds is edged with a border of pure white pebbles. At the highest point of the rock garden is a trellis from which empty bottles hang on ropes; wine bottles, cola bottles, dark beer bottles and the occasional gin bottle. Is this simply an eccentric construction, decoration, like the hub caps nailed all over the fence, or does it serve some purpose unknown to me?

Do Cor and Karel live somewhere near here perhaps? I could scarcely get my bearings as we drove through the night. I look out across the meadows over the low fence. Here and there a white footbridge links the banks of the slightly wider ditches sunk in the low-lying countryside. Cows graze, all with their backs in the same direction. The shadows of clouds float slowly over the grassland towards a line of low houses in the distance, a village that with its silent silhouette, which ends at the left in a church with a square wooden clocktower, seems familiar. I feel I have been here before, know the area, have trudged over those bridges, skated along the narrow, winding ditches, now full of waterweed and stewing in the sun.

I walk slowly along the course of the fence. In a corner full of heaps of sawn-off branches, between which high clumps of stinging nettles are springing up, is a wooden shed. A heart-shaped hole has been cut out at the top of the door. I know that shed too. I lift the latch.

'The throne!'

I don't expect any ducks to be swimming below me now. With a smile I drop my trousers, sit down and listen to the dry fall of excrement, rustling as though rolling through leaves down below, and mumble the word 'latch'. I managed it, although I have some trouble joining the last -ch to the preceding letters. 'Lat-ch.'

A word from a vanished time. It only occurred in my childhood, my boy's hand knew the latch of my own house, of the back doors of houses where my friends lived and where you had to take off your clogs or pattens in the porch before being allowed in in your stockinged feet. A latch. You lifted it up. You didn't raise it, no, you lifted it!

I wipe myself with an old cloth lying next to the hole. Then I pull up my trousers.

I leave the hut. The throne. Behind it are two spindly birch trees. Their leaves hang thinly and breathlessly downwards. I lie down in the grass under the trees. Yes, how often have I lain like this, with a blade of grass between my teeth looking at the scudding clouds, too lazy even to see camels or lions in them. I see a lark above a meadow where something gleams (a sliver of glass?), and suddenly know for certain a world exists, somewhere – I hear its dizzy, soaring song – a world where nothing will ever change, where I shall always remain who I am, scrubbing Uncle Daan's baking trays or listening to the tinkling of the shop bell in our hall while I do my homework at the table, pressing a sugar lump against my palate and feeling it dissolve into sharp grains in my mouth.

The pain in my back gradually subsides. I spread my arms in the grass. My left hand recoils in alarm when my fingers touch a stinging nettle. All the connections have been restored. I put my smarting fingertips into my mouth and suck them, slowly and sensuously.

I'm woken by someone touching me, prodding me gently and enquiringly with his foot, as a dog would with its nose. Then I see the old man. He's holding a small blue enamelled milk churn by a handle in his right hand, just like the one we had at home. With his free hand he strokes his thin grey hair thoughtfully. The sun shines through his large, protruding ears. He looks on appreciatively as I scramble to my feet, plucking some blades of grass from my trousers.

'Pure happiness,' he says loudly as though he were yards away from me. 'Come on,' he continues in the same loud tone, 'a mug of milk will do you good.'

I walk to his cottage with him. The door is open. He invites me in with an expansive gesture as though it were a palace. He's wearing black corduroy trousers and a denim shirt covered in gleaming metal buttons.

The mess in the garden is continued inside. Watering cans, rakes, a washboard, a gent's bike frame, a box full of plugs, empty bottles and tins of all shapes and sizes are scattered over the floor. At the only window is a white-painted kitchen table with two chairs. The old man puts the churn on the table, motions me to sit and walks to a corner of the room where I notice a tap between piles of plates and half-opened packets and boxes of groceries. The man rummages about among the plates, pulls out an earthenware mug and rinses it off under the tap with his fingers. The hut smells unmistakably of goats, an acrid smell which makes one's eyes water.

He puts the white mug on the table in front of me. Twisting and turning he pulls the sunken lid off the metal churn. The sucking sound with which the lid finally comes off immediately takes me back to our kitchen, to Mum, who holds the churn in both hands at an angle over a saucepan on the stove and pours the foaming bluish milk into it.

The old man dips the mug into the churn and sets it down dripping in front of me on the table. He motions me to drink. He seems to be a man of few words. When I have downed the milk, he immediately refills the mug. The milk leaves a fatty deposit on my palate. I smack my lips a few times. The old man smiles, treats the sound as a compliment to the quality of his milk. When I have finished the second mug too, he screws the lid back on the churn and lifts it off the table on to the ground. His hands are covered in great red blotches.

'Well,' he says. 'That was quite a business.' He says nothing and looks at me closely, his hands in front of him on the table. 'How did it happen?'

'Kees Zomer,' I say. 'Dumped into the dark. From driving. A vehicle belonging to two brothers, Karel and Cor. Know?'

'Come again?'

I sigh deeply a couple of times. I must concentrate so that comprehensible sentences come out, not all these fragments.

'Kees Zomer,' I begin again. 'Karel and Cor.' But how do I go on? The story becomes impossible to tell the moment I try to introduce a causal link. 'In the middle of the night got rid of, you see?'

Now the old man opposite me nods, as though he has

74

finally understood. His deep-set blue eyes look at me benevolently.

'They call me IJe* here,' he cries. I put out my hand.

'With sincere appreciation,' I say. 'You discovered me, transported me and pulled me all the way here, didn't you? What a laborious task!'

IJe's look seems to say he finds it quite natural that he should have taken me with him.

'What's your name?'

Perhaps he missed it the first time. My name now comes out more and more fluently.

'Well, well,' says IJe. 'Well, well. Perhaps it's me. I'm a bit deaf, you see. But I didn't understand what you just said to me.'

Don't point to your head now, although that's where the cause lies. 'My speech has become slippery because of a kind of accident. Gone wrong. Thoughts can no longer be converted into aloud. Only inside does everything go smoothly.'

I can see that he doesn't understand me. Or can't he hear me? For a while he surveys me, slowly nodding as if pondering a solution to the communication problem. Then he gets up and walks over to a cupboard with a pile of books on it. He produces a writing pad and a ballpoint pen from a drawer.

'You're an odd one,' he says returning to the table smiling. His toothless mouth opens and he screws up his eyes into slits. 'IJe has been as deaf as a post for years. But I read what people say to me from their lips. Not what you say, though. I can't get the hang of it. Perhaps you can write it down for me?'

* Pronounced 'ay-e'.

75

He pushes the writing pad and the pen towards me. I shake my head.

'Kees Zomer,' says IJe. 'I understand that much. But how did you come to be lying there? I was on my way to the old mill a bit further on with my cart. They're knocking it down. I was going to see if there was anything left for me. And there you lay. No blood or anything. Just unconscious.'

'A receiver. To carry around neck. Did you see anything like that lying there in passing?'

To back up what I'm saying I point to an old bakelite radio on a wooden shelf to one side of the door.

'Found that too,' says IJe. 'They all want new-fangled stuff these days. Transistor radios and suchlike.'

I nod enthusiastically and point to my neck, but I see that he can't make the connection with what I have just said. He taps the writing pad with his finger again.

'That ability has also slipped,' I say.

Something seems to dawn on him. He pulls the notepad towards him and writes something in large, regular, sloping letters. Then he turns the pad round. I recognize the writing. My parents wrote like this. Copperplate. I learned it at school too, in an exercise book with those faint grey lines which you had to keep inside with your dip pen. I recognize the writing but not the words, the letters. I shrug my shoulders helplessly.

'Then you didn't get very far,' concludes IJe.

'Started well, didn't go on. Spoiled. By something.'

I look around helplessly, trying to steer the conversation in a comprehensible direction and searching for my cue. I point to the pile of books.

'Once,' I say. 'I've got lots. Piles! But nothing. Forgotten everything in them. Gone.'

IJe nods. 'Book learning,' he sneers. 'Truth's outside, in nature.'

'Of course,' I agree. 'Spoke for itself.'

'I know people,' the old man continues. He rubs his cheeks, which are full of tiny burst blood vessels. Milkman's cheeks, as Dad always said. You get them from living outdoors. Milkman's cheeks and a neck like a ploughed field. A burnt-up neck. That was what grandfather called it.

'They're pig-headed,' says IJe. 'They chase everything that's new. That's how they get themselves into debt. And who profits from it? The banks!'

He looks at me triumphantly. Outside a cow moos. I look at my watch, but the figures won't make any sense. IJe gets up. He takes a pile of books off the cupboard and puts it on the table. 'You can have them,' he says. 'A present. Take them with you. There's no cure for stupidity.' He stops in the middle of the cluttered room, then walks to a door in the side wall and opens it.

'Here,' he says. 'They came last week. Took all the goats away. Official decision.' He motions me to join him.

The room next to his is full of straw. In a corner is a wooden bed with an untidy pile of blankets on it.

'This is where they slept,' he says. 'Just like me. Why should a man be different from the beasts of the field? It's all pride.'

There are heaps of chopped straw all round him.

'I had to sign forms. To say I was surrendering the animals in the interest of public health. Well, you know what that means, straight to the incineration plant. You can't fool me. I grabbed those papers and tore them to pieces in front of them. Like that.'

He repeats the gesture with his blotchy hands. Despite

77

the emotion visible in his face his voice sounds flat and monotonous.

'Not angrily. Very calmly. First into two, then into four.'

The stall window is covered with brown smudges. A few flies are walking across the glass. I nod and turn away from him so as not to have to comment on his story. IJe comes up to me.

'I'll show you the sheds outside,' he says grimly as if talking to a veterinary inspector. 'They weren't treated better by anybody than by IJe.' He turns round and grabs me by the shoulder. 'It's all pride. On Sundays in church they preach love of your fellow man, compassion, tolerance, or whatever fine words they use these days, but in practice you have to be just like them. Outside everything neatly raked over, front door locked and the curtains closed. But inside . . .' He sniffs in contempt.

He walks ahead of me across the smallholding, between the piles of planks and goat sheds. He stops at each shed and says the names of the confiscated goats: Flora, Mia, Sonia, Antje, Frederika. I feel sorry for him. He seems to guess what I'm thinking.

'Oh, I'll get by,' he says. 'But people, people can't be trusted.'

He stops at a sawhorse. There is some fresh sawdust on the ground. Under the block is a tin bath, an old-fashioned washtub with a handle welded on each side.

IJe walks on, but I seem rooted to the spot. The tub speaks to me, takes me back to Saturday evenings in the kitchen when I was put in the bath by Mum or Dad. I always hoped it would be Mum because in Dad's hands the flannel seemed to turn into sandpaper. When I finally lay upstairs in bed, all aglow in clean cotton pyjamas, my groin would still be stinging. Downstairs the water in the bowl sloshed as they took turns in the tub after me. Sometimes I heard the dirty water running away into the drain next to the kitchen door afterwards, but usually I'd already fallen asleep.

I bend down, stroke the smooth edge of the tub with my finger. It looks like ours. But everyone had a tub like that in those days. As my fingers touch the smoother metal I whisper, 'tub, washtub'. The thing gives its name back to me. My eyes fill with tears. I dry my cheeks with a wild gesture when I see IJe coming, his hands in the pockets of his black corduroy trousers.

IJe stops by the sawhorse. He also seems to be looking at the grey tub with its thin layers of windswept sawdust.

I have to free myself from the tub, from objects that try to drag me back to my childhood. Strange how powerful they are! The milk churn, the tub, the pump. Like magnets. I mustn't give in to their attraction. I must resist, look in a different way, find the key to the moment not so long ago when everything went haywire. That moment is somewhere in my head. I want to find it, but my conscious memory won't take me there, constantly veers off down side tracks. Now there's this tub gleaming and luring me on.

'They're knocking things down all over,' I hear IJe say. 'The mill, and now a bit further on, on the other side of the canal, Sitze's farm. These days they'd rather knock something down than do up the old place. You have to move with the times, they say. But they don't understand that they're sawing off the branch they've been sitting on all their lives. Their own times. Moving with the times. Don't make me laugh.'

He slaps the sawhorse with the flat of his hand.

'In any case they help me keep nice and warm in

winter. There's wood everywhere just waiting to be picked up these days. Are you hungry?'

That question jerks me back into the present, to my stomach which contracts when it hears the word. I nod. I follow IJe to his hut. But instead of going in, he locks the padlock on the door with a large key. I see myself reflected in the convex grey glass of the television screen.

'Can you see yourself?' asks IJe.

I nod.

'That's why it's there. A long time ago it worked. That is, you saw all kinds of programmes about what was happening in the world. But they were never about here. When it broke, I put it outside. People laughed at me, but since then I've got a television which is about my life, and I can appear on it whenever I like.'

He walks slowly back to his cart on the cinder path. He has heavy mid-calf black boots on. There isn't an ounce of fat on his sinewy torso. I move alongside him on his right, no longer afraid of losing sight of the world on the left-hand side.

'I expect you find it strange here, don't you?'

I shake my head, but I can see that this time he wants a verbal answer from me.

'One's own environment is primary.' I hastily bundle some words together.

'What?'

I point to the meadows around us. 'There is no other but this,' I say.

'No other what?'

This time he's read my lips, but hasn't understood what I mean. I must try to express myself more clearly, more concretely. 'These melons are superior to television transmission.'

'Watermelons?' IJe looks around to see whether my words can really change the meadows into melons.

'A sliver of the word gone. I know it really. Let me have a quiet look for it.'

I can see the word in front of me, my mouth forms the letters, tastes them with pursed lips, but won't release them all. When I open my mouth 'melons' comes out again.

But IJe has lost interest in my struggle. He bends down and takes hold of the pull bar of the cart.

'Come on, we'll go and get something to eat,' he says.

I walk next to the cart. IJe's house is in the lee of a dike. We're walking along the raised dike road. To our left a wide ditch, which IJe calls the 'canal', winds its way through the lines of reeds. On the other side of the water there are some farms here and there. A crested grebe dives as we approach. IJe points to the water.

'He's swimming along with us under water,' he says. 'You'd think he'd swim in exactly the opposite direction, but his curiosity gets the better of him. They've got used to people, just like dogs. Become tame.'

When the bird pops up again a little further on it does indeed look as if it's waiting like a dog for us to reach it in order to dive and swim ahead of us a little way.

Some coots are scratching about among the reeds. The black heads with the white spot above the beak nod excitedly as they slide hurriedly into the water.

When we reach a high white footbridge we cross the canal. Chicken bridge, I can hear Dad's voice say in my head, very clearly, so clearly that I have to stop myself glancing round. I help IJe pull the cart on to the bridge. I can feel that I walked like this with Dad, bent forward and trying to add my boy's strength to the pulling of the heavily laden cart. Once we have reached the flat central part of the bridge IJe puts the pull bar on the ground. With our hands on the railing we look out over the countryside, bare, unprotected and low-lying with its rows of trees and mills beneath the scudding clouds. Here and there a ditch glitters in the landscape, but most have been transformed by waterweed into dark ribbons winding towards the horizon.

'There'll be a sea breeze,' says IJe looking at the clouds. 'In a while. Not yet. These are just the advance warning signs.' He points to the perfectly straight road which runs into the polder on the other side of the canal. 'A bit further that way is Sitze's farm.' He picks up the pull bar again, puts it against his back as we carefully shuffle off the bridge, leaning into the bar.

'Counterweight,' I said suddenly, rather proud that this word has popped up at the right moment. But IJe hasn't heard me. His boots are scraping over the tarmac. I look round. There are no shops anywhere. I wonder where IJe is going to go shopping.

'To the shop?' again a fluent, comprehensible sentence, even if it's a bit on the short side. Obviously nothing is possible for the time being except truncated sentences.

'What?' asks IJe.

I want to say shop, but this time department store comes out.

IJe laughs. 'I've never been in a department store, lad. IJe has worked for years without using money. Just like in the war. You trade one thing for another. It works just as well. A few years ago I had a burglary and they took all my money. You should have put it in the bank, IJe, people said. Well, I'd sooner give it away. It's the banks that egg the farmers on to buy more expensive machines, more and more modern farms. Like Sitze.'

IJe points to a farm of which only the front façade is

left standing, buttressed by beams and tall scaffolding. In the farmyard there are two buttercup-yellow skips piled with planks and rubble. IJe pushes the cart ahead of him into the farmyard in the direction of the two bulging skips. He carefully starts examining the contents. Every so often he pulls a plank out of the mess, which for some reason or other seems to be right for something, and puts it in his cart. Suddenly he lifts a gleaming silver birdcage triumphantly from the skip. 'That's our board paid for!' he shouts loudly across the deserted farmyard.

He carries the cage carefully in front of him. 'That'll cost you a lot in the shop,' he says, putting the cage into the cart. I look at the cage with its open doors and the two horizontal perches. Fortunately this object doesn't speak to me. It is free of meaning, it doesn't want anything from me, it's simply what it is.

IJe calls me. He is now standing by the other skip. 'Come and give me a hand!'

I walk over to him.

'Careful,' he says. 'You grab the other end.'

He has the bottom of a glass door in his hands. The frosted glass is decorated with elegantly curling French lilies winding up the length of the wooden frame. In the centre a bouquet of roses is engraved in the glass. The dull white contours are reminiscent of frost flowers the moment before they start melting on your bedroom window. I grab the top of the door. We lift it carefully out of the skip. The door between Dad's shop and the back of the house. When I'm sitting at table eating my porridge I see Dad's outline, busy restocking the shop, shovelling flour or beans from hemp sacks with a scoop which is round at the back so that it fits exactly into the round holes of the wine-red storage drawers, whose contents are described in white curly letters. Rice. Salt. Sugar. I can see him moving vaguely about in a frame of fleurs-de-lys.

'You idiot, look out!' But it's too late. With the door in my hands I walk straight into a beam sticking out of the skip. The glass shatters into a number of large pieces on the ground. IJe and I are left holding the glassless door between us.

'How disappointing,' I stammer sincerely.

'Couldn't you watch where you were going,' screams IJe. 'Well, you might as well let go of it.'

The door topples on to the skip with a crash.

'Christ Almighty,' he says. 'City folk will kill for those things these days, for a door like that. And you just drop it. You're a dead loss. He can't talk, he can't write and he's obviously incapable of holding anything.' His voice resounds across the yard as if he is informing a crowd of my misdeed. He looks once more at the slivers on the ground and then turns abruptly.

'Come on,' he snaps. He lifts up the pull bar and heads off, walking in the direction of the road. I walk behind the cart, head bent, like a child being punished. A blue pick-up passes us in a wide arc and then turns left on to the dike.

We walk the same way back and then turn right, along the other side of the canal. The birdcage glitters in the sun. It is windy on the dike. IJe is proved right. Sea breeze. The water in the canal ripples. A large dark blue umbrella looms up among the reeds.

IJe turns round, points to the umbrella and then to the cage in the cart. 'Let me do the talking,' he says. That's an unnecessary suggestion. I wouldn't dream of speaking to a total stranger.

IJe pulls the cart past the umbrella which is sheltering a fisherman from the wind. The man is sitting on a low collapsible stool at the water's edge. His float has drifted right in the wind. He jerks it out and swings it low over the water back to the left, where the hook with the wriggling worm again disappears into the water.

IJe puts the cart down. The man looks round. He has a port-wine stain on his right cheek. There are brown leather patches on the elbows of his check jacket. He holds a toothpick between his teeth and raises his dark eyebrows when IJe approaches him with the birdcage in his hand. I stand stiffly next to the cart on the dike as though IJe had told me to.

'What do you want?' says the man suspiciously, looking from IJe to his float.

'Have you had a bite?' enquires IJe, his stentorian voice as inexorable as an ultimatum. He stops next to the man and puts the cage on the ground.

'Some perch,' says the fisherman turning up his nose. To illustrate the point he pulls a keep net next to him out of the water. Two perch are lying across each other in the net.

'Swap you?' asks IJe picking up the cage. He holds it out invitingly to the man on the collapsible stool.

'Nice isn't it? Brand-new, can you see?'

'I haven't got any birds,' said the man dryly. The birthmark on his cheek makes him look cross-eyed.

'It's a beautiful cage though,' says IJe. 'You could get a hundred for it with no trouble.'

The mention of that amount seems to unblock something in the man. For the first time he pays serious attention to the cage.

'You didn't pinch it, did you?' he enquires.

'Word of honour,' says IJe.

From the dike I can see that IJe has won the argument. The fisherman pulls up the net and tips the two lifeless fish on to the grass. IJe bends down and with each hand picks up a perch by the tail. Holding the fish he walks back towards me. He lays them carefully on the bottom of the cart.

As we walk on along the dike, I look round again. The fisherman is sitting motionless next to the empty birdcage staring at his float.

IJe looks at me. A contented grin pulls his wrinkles apart. 'That's the way to do it,' he says. He seems to have forgotten the dropped door.

'Consolidation by exchange,' I say because I am grateful to him for his forgiving attitude.

'You could call it that,' agrees IJe.

I can't understand how IJe can swallow a bony perch like that without teeth. He must have a strong stomach. He just tosses the backbone in an arc over his shoulder; he gulps down all the smaller ones, together with the white flesh, without a second thought.

We are sitting on the ground around a brick oven he has built in a pit. The branches under the stones are still glowing. I pick a bone from between my teeth and flick it away between my thumb and forefinger. We look out over the countryside.

A row of lime trees runs from where we are along a road which is invisible from here. Then the word again wells up in me, irresistibly. 'Windbreak!'

IJe looks at me, wiping his fingers on his black trousers.

I point to the row of limes in the distance and repeat the word.

He nods.

'The wind, yes,' he says and looks at the sky across which black thunderclouds are now moving. 'You can

tell by the plovers. You can hear them calling everywhere. The wind makes them restless. Not seagulls,
they're built for the wind. Look.'

He points to a gull hanging unsteadily above the roof
of his hut.

'They can ride the wind with the best of them. It's just
like music looking at them. The music of the spheres.
That's from a book I've got inside. The music of the
spheres. That's what the book's called.'

Two magpies fly into one of the alder trees and nestle
between the branches rustling noisily. I can see their long
tails bobbing up and down. One of them makes a rattling
sound, the other answers abruptly and almost barkingly.
Their bodies gleam blue-black among the leaves. When
the sound is repeated my hand is already moving
through the air, grasping the narrow handle of the
wooden rattle which Uncle Fred has made for my birthday. As you turn the rattle the thin wooden tongue in the
oblong section moves across the wooden cogwheel more
and more sharply and violently, and then slower and
slower until the wood in the middle jumps from cog to
cog. Tack-tock. Tock-tack.

'What are you doing?'

When I hear the high-pitched child's voice behind me
my hand drops in alarm.

'That's Jules, Melle and Maria's son,' says IJe. The
boy's yellow T-shirt hangs loosely over his jeans. There is
a picture of a laughing moon on it. Under the black
drawing is a word I can't read that moves when the boy
comes closer, his eyes fixed on me.

'Jules has got a hut here, a secret hut. Isn't that right,
Jules?'

The boy nods stiffly. He goes on staring at me, pokes a
forefinger in my direction.

'Who's he?'

'That's Kees. I found him.'

The boy squats down at a safe distance in the grass. He pulls a blade of grass out of the ground and takes it in his teeth.

'Found?'

IJe nods. 'By the side of the road. Unconscious.'

The boy's thin fair hair is brushed aside by the wind. He gets up and puts his hands in his pockets. I can't work out how old he is. I find it odd that I can't. How old am I myself? I'm not sure exactly, but I must be somewhere in my prime. The boy's snub nose bobs up and down for a moment, like a squirrel's.

'Did they beat him unconscious?' he asks.

'I don't know, lad. Ask him yourself.'

The boy plants his feet a little further apart but says nothing. Perhaps he doesn't dare. I can see from his face that he's curious, expecting a story.

I smile at him. Two sparrows fly right overhead. The sound of their wings evokes the word 'whiskers', which my mouth can't keep back. As soon as I've said it, I shake my head in apology.

'I find it difficult. What first, what later. It was night . . .' My voice falters, then finds the rest of the sentence, ''Twas pitch-black night. The robber chief could see no light.'

The child nods. ''Twas night, a pitch-black night,' he repeats in a clear voice. 'I know that story. It never ends. It's really corny.'

'Come on,' says IJe, raising himself on one hand with a groan. 'Show Kees your hut.'

I can see that the boy is hesitating.

'It's a secret hut,' he says to IJe.

'Kees won't give you away. He doesn't know anyone here.'

We follow the boy, who walks on tiptoe between the planks and the empty goat sheds. He stops close to the wooden fence. On the ground in front of his feet is a broken-off section of trellis, which he pushes aside as he squats down. A square hole is revealed, supported at the sides with planks.

'Trap,' I suddenly realize with great certainty. Jules shakes his head.

'This is the hut,' he says. 'No one's allowed inside, except for me.'

The boy jumps into the hole, and pulls the trellis over the opening. Only his shiny blond crown is still visible.

IJe grabs me by my sleeve. We walk back slowly in the direction of his house.

'He's got a chest in his hut,' says IJe. 'He keeps *Robinson Crusoe* in it. I gave him the book a year ago when he'd just learned to read. Since then he's started on the hut.'

IJe stops in front of his rockery. He looks at the bottles on strings, which move gently in the wind but don't touch each other.

'I don't know what he's thinking about,' he says thoughtfully. 'Whether he is sitting in his hut as Robinson or Man Friday. What do you think?'

'What age does he have?' I ask.

'Eight,' says IJe. 'But he's a tough little lad for his age.'

He turns round at the door of his cottage. 'Maybe he's Man Friday one day, and Robinson the next.' He looks at the sky. 'The wind's getting up,' he says contentedly and turns to go inside. 'That's one thing they can't touch. When they've messed everything up, that great wind here will still blow over the countryside. It doesn't give a damn about us people.'

89

He points to the TV screen by the door. 'The weather forecast,' he says. 'Whenever I want. The wind's already getting stronger. If we're lucky you'll be able to hear my organ play in a little while. The music of the spheres. I've got that book indoors.'

Sometimes I'm afraid I no longer understand what people are saying to me. I need to be certain that I at least understand them. That I'm not losing my grasp of what they mean.

I sit down and put my hands on the table. The hut. Robinson Crusoe. Man Friday. I followed all that. The boy in the hut. The wind that IJe is expecting. But how am I to make the connection with an organ, music?

It's quiet. You can't hear the wind inside. IJe has gone into the stall next to his cottage. I stay sitting at the table. If only I still had the transistor. Music orders not only my body but my thoughts too. The worst thing is to be shut up like this inside your life, not able to think any further than your eyes can see. To say nothing of what's past. I remember the glass door with the fleurs-de-lys, the bird-cage next to the fisherman, how IJe cut open the perch with a worn-down potato knife and deftly gutted it, but all those separate snatches no longer form a story. They are floating around my head as fragments, won't form into something you could call the course of a day.

Yes, I can remember. It's better than it was, when it began with nothing at all, but it's not enough. Because if there are no links any more, no sequences, your mem-ories are worthless. Or perhaps those links don't exist. Are they pure imagination, and am I the only person alive who knows? Don't let that be the truth. For God's sake.

I hear snoring coming from the stall. I get up and go outside. Then I hear the sound and understand what IJe meant just now. I hurry to the rockery. The marigolds are waving in the wind. The large and small bottles are swinging on their strings. Following a score that only the wind can read they strike each other, sometimes softly, sometimes harder. The music of the spheres. I look at the wobbling bottles. Ting-ting, say the wine and beer bottles to each other. The afternoon light is reflected brightly in the hub caps on the fence. I walk in the direction of the secret hut. I shuffle cautiously to the edge of the hole, as though that will make the word 'trap', which now forms silently on my lips, materialize right in front of me.

The section of fencing is pushed across the hole, but the boy's blond head beneath it has disappeared. I cautiously pull the trellis aside and look into the trap. There is the wooden box. Supporting myself on the edges, I lower myself into the hole.

I slowly sink to my knees. I pick up the box and put it on my lap. When I have taken the book out, I put the box aside and open the book using my raised knees as a rest.

It's an old book, I can see that from the typeface they have used, and from the engravings of course. I sniff the threadbare light blue binding, but the smell of glue has long since vanished and been replaced by that of earth and half-rotted leaves. I look at page after page, but not one word, not even a letter will give up its secret. It remains printed matter, as void of meaning as a page of Chinese calligraphy.

I know the book. I must have read it as a boy. The writer is called Daniel Defoe and the book first appeared in 1719, when Defoe was fifty-nine (I don't know how I have come by this knowledge).

I look closely at the engravings, which illustrate the climaxes in the story. The shipwreck, the building of the hut, fishing with a home-made rod, making fire by striking two rocks against each other, the shirt at the top of the highest tree, the sailing ship which glides past on the horizon without noticing the shipwrecked sailor waving on the beach.

The engravings have been done precisely and without much imagination, typical nineteenth-century crafts-manship. Then my eyes are caught by one picture, and can't tear themselves away from it: Man Friday's foot-steps in the sand along the shoreline of the desert island. The tracks are large and clear, the edges of the footprints have been shaded to suggest depth. Robinson himself isn't in the picture, so that the person looking at it becomes Robinson for a moment, staring with heart pounding at the traces of another living being, a fellow creature that he will go in search of and will find.

However, I also remember another story, a variant. In that story Robinson mistakes his own tracks for those of someone else, the hallucinatory beginning of a progress-ive madness which will finally drive him into the water and to death by drowning.

I scan the right-hand page next to the illustration. His name must be somewhere among all those letters. Friday. I let the word resound through my head. I don't admit any other word to my thoughts as I scan line by line. Then, just over halfway through, I find it. I don't recog-nize it – at least that's not how it feels – but something in me points, as if with an arrow, to one word among all those other words. I stare at it for minutes on end until it has separated itself from the page and has etched itself in my mind as a graphic image. When I close my eyes I can see the picture of the word glowing in the darkness.

I close the book, with its lettering stamped in board in which fragments of gold leaf have stuck, put it back in the box and climb out of the hole.

Two seagulls flutter close to the ground in front of me and then dive over the fence into the meadows. The sun hangs above the horizon in the west.

The door of IJe's cottage is open. I walk in and hear the old man's familiar snoring in the room next door. I take the writing pad and the ballpoint pen from the drawer of the oak chest on which the pile of books is lying. I sit down at the table, look straight ahead for a moment. A white, almost transparent spider, its legs thrashing about, is lowering itself on a thread from the ceiling to the table. Then my hand transfers the signs from my head to the white paper. At first laboriously, but gradually faster and more fluently. Friday, I think, every time I write the word down. Friday. It looks like lines written as a punishment in school, but it's not that at all. Friday. Friday.

In the stall I hear IJe cough a few times. Then he lets out a deep sigh and a little later I hear his shoes shuffling through the straw to the door.

IJe holds on to the doorpost with one hand. He stretches, so that his denim shirt slips out of his trousers on one side.

'Do you want some coffee?' he calls in a voice still hoarse with sleep. 'Coffee?'

I nod with the writing pad in front of me on the table. IJe fills a battered kettle with water and fishes an electric hotplate out of an open box on which the bicycle frame rests. He pushes the plug into the socket.

He stands looking at me with his back to the bicycle frame. Then he raises his left forefinger.

'In a little while the water will start singing,' he says. He whistles softly, reinforcing the sound that the water in the kettle will soon be making.

'I can't hear it,' he says, turning round and looking at

the kettle on the hotplate. 'At first all I see are wisps of steam escaping from the kettle, then it turns into a jet, whiter and whiter, stronger and stronger. And then, suddenly, I hear the water roaring. Do you understand why that is, Kees?'

I nod. I know why that is. But can I explain it to him? My hands grip the edge of the table.

'The high-pitched notes make the eardrum vibrate,' I say. 'Understood? Get? Low remains dead, but up high you hear music.' And now I too whistle along with the water, which is coming to the boil.

IJe seems to understand me. As he puts Nescafé into two mugs and pours boiling water over it, he says, 'Just like I can hear some birds and not others. Ducks and geese I can't, larks and plovers I can.'

I nod. 'As clear as crystal.'

IJe sits down opposite me. He observes the transparent spider scrambling over the edge of the table and then dropping to the ground on a newly spun thread while he stirs his coffee with a finger. Is that why his fingers look so blotchy and red?

I look timidly at his calm face, the wrinkled skin of the neck beneath it, taut in the middle round the protruding Adam's apple. His lips have a bluish glow. Then I turn the writing pad round and push it slowly across the table towards him.

He raises his eyebrows and bends over the paper. Then he says loudly and clearly, 'Friday. Friday. And Friday again. And again and on and on. That's right. Today's Friday.'

I grab his arm. Tears well up. I point wildly to the words and then to my right hand.

'So can you write after all?'

First I nod, then I quickly shake my head.

'Perhaps. If one sheep leaps over the ditch.' Proverbs come out just as easily as ever.

'The rest will follow,' IJe adds. He's following my thoughts. Now I must make sure I don't get too excited, and get things confused again. I nod fervently. He pushes the pad back.

The strange thing is that *I* can't read this word, this endlessly repeated Friday. But the knowledge that it's there, that IJe has recognized it and spoken it makes me happy.

When I look at IJe again I can see his left cheek and eye repeated in space next to his face. It reminds me of the colours of a cartoon in the paper carelessly printed over the black edges. A stabbing pain in my neck makes me grab my head.

'You're as pale as a ghost, mate,' says IJe and gets up. 'Come on, you should lie down for a bit.'

He holds my hand as he takes me to his bed. As I drop on to the bed I can feel myself sinking.

When I wake up it's dark. There is a faint light from the open door. I seem to hear music outside. I raise myself on my elbows with a groan. I can place the sounds now. In the rising wind the bottles outside in the rockery are clinking and jingling against each other. I sink back again and listen to the wind playing IJe's bottle organ, sometimes subtly and ethereally and then swelling in a wildly jingling crescendo.

My head feels lighter, as though my blood pressure has dropped. I let my legs dangle out of the bed and then carefully stand up.

In the doorway I see IJe sitting at the table. In the corner of the room next to the oak chest there is a table lamp with its pink shade hanging askew. On the table there is some cake and a knife. IJe turns his head in my direction.

'Honky-tonk,' I say pointing in the direction of the dark window.

The table lamp throws a round pool of light on to the ceiling in which two flies buzz round each other.

'Like I told you,' says IJe. 'The wind. It doesn't usually blow as hard as this at this time of year. Want a piece of cake?'

I join him at the table, rubbing my cheeks.

'High notes. Like the steam,' I say.

'What?'

'That glass music outside.'

IJe doesn't hear me. He's absorbed in the job of cutting a slice of cake.

I put the piece in my mouth, munch and feel something crack between my teeth. Then I taste the crystallized candy as it splits open and see them again hanging under the kitchen shelf, chains of sweets, the brown, half-transparent smooth crystal surfaces of Mum's home-made sweets.

'Candy,' I say. 'Classic sweet.'

'Yes, candy cake,' says IJe. 'I sometimes get some from Maria, Jules's mother. She thinks I'm short of everything.'

He laughs. I see the smooth, deep-red gums, the rasping tongue which pokes out for a second and then withdraws into the toothless mouth.

'They're having a rough time out at sea now,' he shouts and stands up. He walks over to the chocolate-brown radio on the shelf next to the door and turns it on.

And just as I used to, before the Paul Temple signature tune came on and a new episode began, I hear first the hissing of the slowly warming radio valves. Then gently and distantly at first a voice glides into the room. IJe turns the volume up full. It's as though the newsreader is in the room. IJe stays by the blaring radio. The newsreader is talking about the raising of camping fees, poisoned drinking water and a car accident in which two people have been killed. Then another voice takes over from him and reads the weather forecast. Strong to gale-force winds dying out during the night. IJe nods contentedly and turns the radio down. Immediately after the weather forecast music starts playing.

'Music,' he says. 'It's pretty awful having to do without that. Particularly Verdi. Giuseppe Verdi. I miss his music. Sometimes I try to remember the arias, but it's ridiculous, I can't recall the music. As though I'm deaf inside too.'

'When I was half, it helped me get on in the world, music,' I say. 'Greater than power of words. Just accept that from me.'

He doesn't look at my lips and so he can't hear what I am saying. He seems to be lost in his own thoughts.

'Music of the spheres!'

IJe gets up, walks over to the books on the chest and pulls one out from the bottom of the pile. He places it on the table in front of him, and leafs through it.

'This is all about the opera. All opera composers. Verdi. Puccini. Berlioz. I thought he was wonderful too, that Berlioz.'

He pushes the book towards me. Greedily my eyes scan the letters. I can scarcely conceal my disappointment. I can't recognize a word. I push the book abruptly back across the table.

'Let's go to bed,' says IJe, the piece of cake in his hand.

When we are in bed, he in the wooden bed, and I on

some blankets in another corner of the stall, we listen to the wind howling through the roof tiles, to the jingling bottles outside in the garden.

'I can hear that,' says IJe in the dark. 'The wind in the bottles. But it never plays one of Verdi's tunes. The wind can't do that, make tunes.'

I don't answer. I can't reach him in the dark anyway.

'Come on,' says IJe, tapping his finger on the sheet of paper that I filled with words yesterday.

'Friday,' I say and take a gulp of the bitter Nescafé.

'That was yesterday,' he says, 'so today it's . . .?' He's talking as if I'm a child. I sneak a glance at my watch, as though the answer to his question is there.

'Monday,' says IJe. 'Monday, Tuesday, Wednesday.'

I can feel my lips moving along with the names of the days, and then I join in, 'Thursday, Friday, Saturday, Sunday.'

'Exactly,' says IJe. 'You see, you remember.'

'Forgotten,' I say. 'But now you say them: in order!'

'On Saturdays I'm always allowed to take a shower in the cemetery,' says IJe.

I look at him in bewilderment.

'There are no funerals on Saturday,' he explains. 'So I'm allowed to use the shower in the chapel of rest.'

'Ugh,' I say. 'Really creepy.'

'You stink pretty bad come to that, my friend.' IJe laughs.

Only now do I realize that I obviously can't smell myself any more. Just as I've begun to regard my stubbly beard as a natural extension of my face. I sniff the sleeve of my shirt, but all I can smell is straw. Straw and the acrid scent of goats.

'Billy goat,' I say. 'I smell of billy goat.'

The wind has died down. It's still early, the sun is still low in the sky and there is a fine mist around the high feet of the electricity pylons. I remember that from summer mornings, walks we took on Sunday mornings around the village while Dad looked mockingly at the churchgoers in black on the dike. Maybe it's that row of swallows on an electricity cable that evokes this image in me: earnest people in black, goose-stepping along the dike on the way to the church with its chiming bell.

Now the bell is hanging silently in its wooden cage. The square tower is painted dark green, like the church tower in our village. IJe's shoes clump down the road. He greets the people we meet with a broad wave. They look at us curiously.

'They want to know who you are. Everybody knows everybody here. But I don't want any part of it. I don't want anything to do with them. They've taken all my goats. I know exactly what they say behind my back. They think I'm mad. Maria and Melle are the only ones who don't. They know me. They know I've lived all my life on this land. Sometimes here, sometimes there. You were a farmhand. There was nothing else. From one farmer to the next.'

A woman cycles up behind us. She looks round as she passes us and almost loses control of the steering as she makes the manoeuvre.

'Serves her right,' says IJe. 'Come on, let's take this path. Then we can skirt the centre. I don't like going into the village if I don't have to. They're already gossiping about who you are. Gossip spreads like wildfire here.'

The narrow path runs along a ditch. There are pieces of newspaper and plastic everywhere under the bushes by the water's edge. In one of the pollarded willows on the other side of the ditch is a single moped wheel. IJe points to it.

'Those are the signs of their civilization. You should always look at the outside, the edge of a village, then you know at once what it's like inside. Lots of fuss about nothing and mounds of rubbish, that's society these days. Recently they had to demolish a whole street of new buildings. It turned out they'd built them on a toxic waste dump. No one knew about it. Except for Joris de Goede, that is, who'd sold the ground to the council in the first place. Now they're trying to find out who dumped the rubbish there and how much De Goede made out of it. But of course there are no papers, just as there's no money left.'

We walk past the back of a terrace of low houses, their wooden fronts painted grey. Washing hangs out to dry in the gardens. A naked child sits in a red inflatable pool and slaps the water with the palms of its hands. A blackbird perches on a television aerial, motionless as a weather vane.

The path curves right at the gate of the cemetery. I look through the bars at the upright headstones. Most of them are old and weathered.

'I'm curious to know if they'll have me here in a little while,' says IJe. 'I don't hold with that new-fangled cremating. People should be put back in the earth, if you ask me.'

I nod. We walk round the railings with their gilded points. The entrance to the cemetery is right next to the church door. The sun is shining into the leaded lights of the church windows.

'Right,' says IJe, stepping on to the gravel path. His tone suggests that we have reached our destination. Our shoes crunch along the path. I assume that this is where

IJe got the white pebbles he used to decorate his bed of marigolds. Most of the dead have been here for a long time. I can't see fresh flowers anywhere. IJe points to a red-brick hut that is more or less in the middle of the cemetery, right against the railings. It looks like a small electricity sub-station, except that there's no picture of a skull on the metal door.

'I'll go first,' says IJe. He looks round the cemetery. 'The young people are leaving, they die everywhere but here.' He pulls the door open and goes inside.

The gravel pricks painfully through the thin soles of my shoes. So I walk on the verges, though I suspect that that's precisely what the notices stuck here and there in the grass are telling me not to do. Most of the graves are simple and alike: a raised headstone with a piece of grass or gravel framed in black stone in front. The old graves are at the back. Here the stones are flat on the ground. Fine grey moss has nestled in the carved letters. I squat down in front of one of the stones. With the fingers of my right hand I slowly feel the shape of the raised letters one by one. My fingers read, then suddenly stiffen, then go on feeling quickly over the chilly surface. I stand up. My knees are shaking and hurting, can scarcely bear the weight of my body any more when I read the name on the stone in front of me, now just with my eyes.

I turn round and run from the cemetery. The village is in front of me. A long street with houses on both sides and a few shops. The Bovenweg.

I slow down. I must enter the village unobtrusively. As though I'm really dead, like Kees Tol lying there behind me in the cemetery; as though the people in the street can't see me as I see them, as I recognize them.

Four

Miss Tersteeg, who always comes to the door when I collect a prescription for Mum from Dr Verhulst or some linctus for Hanna who has whooping cough, enters the gate in front of the doctor's tall house and pushes open the oak door. The heavy door closes behind her, slowly and inexorably.

I also walk along the paved path to the front door. In the garden behind the house the reddish brown leaves of the beech tree shiver as if welcoming me. I stop in front of the slate step which Miss Tersteeg scrubbed early this morning. The rustling beech leaves want me to go through the door, to give up everything that I am. Come back, they breathe. Push the door open with both hands, boy, they lisp. Disappear for ever in the cool interior. That's what they whisper.

I read the raised black lettering on the white marble plate next to the door. 'Dr. L. T. Vrolijk. By appointment only.' I read it twice, three times. It's so simple, so natural, as though the helplessness with which I stared at the pages of a book was nothing but imagination. I read the text on the plate, time after time. It's as if a memory dissolves before my eyes into a present action, telling me that Dr Verhulst is now called Dr Vrolijk.

I walk down the side of the doctor's house. The wrought-iron bars in front of the cellar windows are the same as they were. And the tap in the outside wall, a little further on, to which Dr Verhulst's wife, a short woman in a trouser suit, connects the green garden hose now coiled next to the rain barrel.

I lift the lid of the heavy barrel by its wooden handle. The round, worn lid meets the flat of my hand. On the still surface a couple of straws float and between them an insect skates energetically back and forth. You don't need to recognize animals, they're always there, always the same, in the same static, animal time.

I read the message of the twitching water creature. It's the same message that the beech leaves whisper in my ear. Give up, just let yourself sink, it's simple. You float round in the barrel, in the same circles on the wafer-thin surface until you sink and disappear into the black depths and another creature, your exact double, takes over your work on the surface. My pale narrow face looms up beneath the skating insect. An unkempt grey beard covers my chin and the bottom half of my cheeks. I smile. No one will recognize me like this. Kees Zomer can walk about here quite calmly without anyone coming up to him and saying, 'Hey, come here, you'.

I put the lid back and walk to the bottom of the garden. Beneath the beech tree there is a set of white, cast-iron garden furniture, a table, two chairs and a bench. On the table there is an open book whose flapping pages beckon me invitingly. Heart pounding, I walk towards the book. The sound of the leaves above my head directs my eyes along the lines, catches them on the right-hand side of the page and the rustling brings them back to the beginning of the following line. I read to the rhythm of the music, though what I read doesn't get through to me. The joy of reading itself surpasses any meaning. Words string themselves together into sentences and divide into main and subordinate clauses. My eyes follow the points of the punctuation. A noun looks for a verb, conjugates it (and remember how to spell the ending, whispers Mr Van Tricht, the schoolmaster), a subject is given its predicate. Then it's the turn of the auxiliary verbs. And then the subordinate clauses, one after the other, which divide, and melodically, fuller and fuller and more persuasively, echo the leaves above my head.

At the bottom of the garden there is a chicken bridge with a gate in the middle which divides the doctor's garden from the school playground. (How many children with grazed knees and bloody elbows have been taken sobbing to the doctor's house over that bridge?)

The heels of my shoes rest against the cross-slats of the bridge's sloping planks, my hand lifts the iron latch of the gate. I walk over the bridge across the ditch filled with waterweed and reach the silent flagstone playground, in the corner the bicycle racks with their corrugated iron roof where we gathered among the bikes when the rain pounded on the roof and Mr Van Tricht lit the round white hanging lamps inside one by one.

The school playground is abandoned now, the bicycle racks are empty and in the stone building, with the date 1912 in raised letters on its façade, there is no light. I hesitate for a moment, confronted with the facts, then I cross the playground. I hear the girls screaming as they play tag, the thudding of one jumper into the back of the previous jumper in leapfrog, the scrape of iron-tipped shoes as boys run about, the clatter of wooden clogs and the swish of the skipping rope in the skipping area next to the open school doors, where Mr Van Tricht and Miss Asselbergs stand side by side watching us until it is time to march back in again in two files, boys and girls separately, into the classrooms smelling of chalk dust and sponge boxes and damp coats which hang drying over the semi-circular stove guard perforated with holes.

I look at the third desk in the middle row, where I am sitting writing on my slate with the hard point of the grey pencil while Mr Van Tricht puts a pencil in the pencil sharpener screwed to the edge of his desk. As the point of the pencil gets sharper and sharper the sharpener gives a higher and more contented hum.

It is quiet around me. Only the scratching of the slate pencils can be heard while the voice of Mr Van Tricht repeats the last words of the dictation: 'The besieged townspeople seemed unaffected by the repeated attacks of the deceitful enemy.'

Like Mr Van Tricht I repeat the sentence aloud a couple of times as I walk past the school building to the gate. I turn the round handle to the right. The languid click with which the gate closes behind me means that I don't have to stay behind in detention to write lines, the same line again and again, that same statement now welling up from my body and looking for words. I can read, I can read!

Three houses further on is Van Dam's shop.

'Stationery' it says on the shop window and beneath it, in smaller letters, 'and Lending Library'. That's where I get the brown-covered cowboy books for Dad and the large square sixpenny novels by my favourite writer, Hans de la Rive Box. Now other words appear behind it, the word 'Tobacconist' displaces the word 'Stationery' until the latter has vanished, absorbed into the newer, more modern lettering.

I don't recognize the inside of the shop. Because of the rows of cigarette packets in the sloping white compartments, the piles of exercise books, multi-coloured sponge boxes and the slate pencils tied together with shiny red paper in packs of twelve can only vaguely be seen. Next to the till there is a chrome-plated stapler, the only one that managed to make the transition from stationer's to tobacconist's. There is no one in the shop. The cream-coloured sliding doors to the back room are closed. As long as they stay closed, the covered and numbered books in the lending library go on sitting on the wooden shelves behind them.

In the shop window there is an advertisement cut out of cardboard. It's called display today, display material. I can hear the voice of a young man (where from?) enthusiastically pronouncing that word. The picture shows a desert. A caravan of camels passes on the horizon. A pair of hairy man's hands stick out of the sand in the foreground. A blonde in a bikini rushes towards them with a packet of cigarettes in her outstretched hands.

'For adventurous smoking pleasure,' it says in black letters on the tin stand holding the picture. I can read the text easily, but the connection between the text and the illustration escapes me.

Opposite is Peet's shop, where I tried on my first pair of long trousers. My father calls them turd-catchers. When I protest at the name he says that I can call them plus fours if I like.

Mr Peet is still standing in the shop. Or is it someone who looks very much like him? The same thin lips and mobile fingers with which he 'takes' your waist and length measurements, as he puts it.

I walk further down the perfectly straight Bovenweg. The residents still keep their front gardens neat. The carefully raked gravel paths, flowered borders and squared hedges are an extension of the interiors I can see through the bay windows.

In the rooms women wander around with cups of coffee, men sit reading the newspaper in short-sleeved pullovers, a child sits with legs apart on the carpet staring at a red toy car.

A garden gnome stands by a small pond. From some other space the voice of my son Wouter tells me to go on reading. Wouter has never been here. He's the same age as I am just before Dad shuts up shop and we leave the village behind for ever in the roomy cab of Tigchelaar's removal van.

I hurry down the street to reach our shop in time. It's at the other end of the village. I can see from a long way off that I'm too late. The word 'Dairy Products' has already been removed from the window. But the interior with all its drawers, cupboards and sliding glass doors has waited patiently for me. Longing for the smell of freshly roasted coffee from the shiny silver coffee grinder with its brass funnel into which Dad let the coffee beans rattle, I open the shop door. There is no jingling of the bell, or smell of coffee. The shop smells faintly of soap powder now. A man with a bald head and Dad's camel-coloured shop coat comes from the back of the shop. He stops next to a wire carousel of panties packed in plastic. I realize that I can scarcely seem a very attractive customer in his eyes. I must take the initiative, explain my presence here, but suddenly can't think of an opening sentence.

'What can I do for you?' says the man and walks slowly in the direction of Dad's old-fashioned silver-plated till. The inclination to repeat his sentence is so strong that I have to open my mouth as wide as I can and wait until his words are out before I say anything myself.

'Do,' I say, entangled in repetition. 'Do. One swallow

doesn't make a Zomer. Kees Zomer. Called after my father who was also a Zomer.'

'Yes, I understand,' says the man gruffly, resting one hand on the till. 'But what will it be?'

'Where there's a will, there's a way.' Another proverb which is more of a hindrance than a help. On the contrary, these proverbs are taking me further and further from the main point.

'With apologies,' I say. 'My father runs a shop here.'

'Your father?' The man grabs his nose, as if to check if it's still there. He half turns in the direction of the back of the shop and shouts in a high-pitched, nasal voice: 'Rietje!'

A plump woman with bright red lips shuffles from the back of the house in a white sleeveless dress and slippers. Her hair is fastened back with shiny copper pins. She really looks nothing like Mum. I'm close to tears.

'My mother and my father,' I start saying to the woman, but the man interrupts me.

'This gentleman maintains that his father runs a shop here.'

The woman looks from me to her husband.

'Kees Zomer,' I say. 'Surprised to meet you.'

The woman gives a hearty laugh.

'So am I,' she says. 'Because that would make you my son.'

'Stop it, Rietje,' says the man in irritation. 'I've never heard of a Zomer in the village. Have you?'

The woman shakes her head. She is suddenly serious again. She has plucked her eyebrows and this makes her forehead look large and flabby. Her features lack the support of Mum's firm chin. She hugs herself, taking hold of her bare brown upper arms.

'You've made a mistake,' she says. 'What address were you looking for?'

'Fourteen Bovenweg.' That fact is lodged indelibly in my memory and comes out without a hitch.

'This is number twenty. Look on the door outside.'

She walks past me and opens the shop door. I look quickly outside. No shop bell.

I walk out in confusion. I don't dare look round because there are tears in my eyes. I know for certain that the man and the woman are standing side by side in the doorway staring after me.

I walk down the Bovenweg past long rows of greenhouses to the crossroads. Here there is an oblong sign with the name of the village on the back. I no longer need to read the name. There's no point in looking back. I start running.

Five

As I run on between the fields I can feel my body filling with exhaustion. Finally its ever-increasing weight forces me to a halt. It makes itself felt more than ever, even in its furthest recesses, creating a clear-cut distinction between myself and the world.

I lie down on my back at the roadside. For a while I can do no more than gasp for breath, wait until my heart and lungs have regained control over the rest of my body, until thought cautiously reasserts itself to the rhythm of the sharp cries of plovers and the cawing of a group of crows on a ploughed field.

There is great danger in objects. For the first time I understand what the concept of melancholy really means: not pondering on past events, but the awareness of the pervasive presence of the past, lying hidden in things; only touch them and they return, the sounds, the smells, the words and the faces you thought up to now you could shelve under the reassuring heading of 'the past'. Only now do you realize that the past can fool you at any moment, is waiting in your body for its chance like a bacterium. Now melancholy is a sickness which infects you via the objects around you, the present no more than a paper-thin surface and every object a potential hole in it. Because people are unaware that objects belong not only to space but also to time, melancholy seizes its opportunity again and again, the dead and their vanished deeds hang around waiting for the opportunity to re-establish contact with you through an object and drag you into their terrifying realm of pure space, pure absence. Only in a place where all traces of the past have been erased would you be completely safe.

I sit up and look around me. As far as the eye can see, the whole of this low-lying landscape, with its winding, glittering ditches and bridges, dark rectangular fields, scattered mills and straight rows of trees, which hurry to the horizon and there dissolve, as though wanting to be absorbed into light, is covered with a thin layer of varnish. Only one trigger is needed and it will crack. You will tumble head over heels into the dark underpainting which is best avoided during your lifetime, but which, once touched, echoes beneath your real life like the hollow sound beneath the ice that shot away in all directions when you crossed its blue-black expanse all alone on your Frisian skates; a sinister accompaniment to your bold attempt to reach the other side, the stiff, frozen fringes of reeds which marked the beginning of an unknown world. You hear the blades of the little skater moving further away stroke by stroke, the ice crackling towards the sides under the passing weight of the boy's body, which crackles too because of the newspapers under his black woollen sweater, secured with a leather belt. I sit at the roadside and see him reach the other side, disappear among the lines of reeds. Now the boy has disappeared from sight.

I look at the fields, at their stillness, scarcely disturbed by the rasping sound of the grazing black-and-white cows.

Cautiously I savour the past tense in words like 'once',

111

'then', 'last year', 'long ago'. I realize that I am able to, falteringly and slowly, but I am able. I can speak about myself in the past tense, although the recent past is still only present in bursts. I say aloud, 'He got up and walked towards the bike leaning against a fence further on.' Then I do what the sentence has prompted me to do.

I look around, but the owner of the bicycle is nowhere to be seen. The bicycle isn't locked. With one hand on the saddle and one on the handlebars, I push it ahead of me into the road and jump into the saddle.

At a crossroads I find a signpost. I read a word, 'Bergen', that I immediately recognize and turn left towards the edge of a wood. Beyond that must be the mountains the signpost promises me. Only five miles further on I will ride uphill, look out in all directions, finally get an overview.

The distance on the signposts steadily decreases, but the road doesn't climb, as though the surroundings refuse to meet the promises of language.

I am riding down woody avenues. Dappled light flickers ahead of me along the cycle paths and the car traffic is increasing. Many cars have number plates which are unfamiliar. At the last signpost the figure gives way to a horizontal strip. I turn left and follow the cycle path alongside the main road. A long line of cars winds its way slowly between the trees. The stink of exhaust fumes mingles with the smell of pine needles. Then the road widens and to my astonishment I enter a village without warning.

Where has it come from so suddenly? I can't immediately classify it or place it. So I cycle on until I reach a square with a church in the middle. When I ride around the square I can see that only the outside walls of the church are still standing.

I recognize the square with its low houses, the elegantly carved white roof frames along the gables painted in moss green, the flattened cobbles in the old-fashioned street which produce a humming sound from my wheels. The signboards above the shops strike me as familiar, are trying to remind me of earlier events which obviously happened while I was here. One of the shops around the square stands out, almost literally thrusting its front at me. Its window is full of books. I brake, place my bike against the low wall which separates the grave-yard from the road and cross the road between two slowly passing cars. I stand in front of the window for a long time and look at the covers of the books on display. Some of them seem familiar. The names of the writers are a prelude to some knowledge just below the surface of my consciousness. Just as words were a little while ago. I saw the word in front of me, the number of letters, heard the sound of the distinctive vowel, felt my tongue assuming the correct position in my mouth to speak the word. The word was more present in me than it had ever been and yet I couldn't reach it.

The names of the writers on the books trigger series of images. I can see the faces which go with the names, the interior of a light, spacious room with two desks, piled with books and files. I smell the smell of printed paper, hear the binding of a new book crack when opened for the first time.

Now and then people go into the bookshop. Next to the front door is a rack full of newspapers. I can see that it's Saturday 12 August. When I look through the window into the shop, my eyes meet a round, flaccid face which seems astonished to recognize me. The man, dressed in beige trousers and a white short-sleeved shirt, comes towards me energetically, and excitedly pulls me by one arm into the shop. He seems both surprised and pleased to see me. Only when I hear his voice do I recognize him.

'Mr Zomer,' says Richard Fielemieg. 'Mr Zomer. You here?'

'Mr Zomer, you here,' I repeat in the same intonation. He thinks I'm mimicking him, pulling his leg perhaps, but that's all my power of speech is capable of at this moment. I try not to listen to what a man and a woman are saying to each other at the back of the shop, frightened of having to repeat their sentences too.

With a friendly smile he pulls me towards the counter, where a woman with white hair and white eyebrows is busy wrapping a book.

'Look who's here, Rita. Mr Zomer from Discus Publishers.'

The woman stares at me with watery eyes as though I'm a ghost. Her fingers let go of the inward-folding triangular corners of the wrapping paper.

I smile hesitantly and extend my hand to the woman. Richard Fielemieg is right. I know, but I can't yet give any content at all to this qualification which I've been assigned, and which feels like a signboard hanging in a vacuum, Discus Publishers.

'Where have you been all this time?'

I hear myself repeating his question. He's not smiling now.

'What do you mean? In the shop of course.'

'What do you mean? In the shop of course.'

I take a couple of steps backwards, as though trying to distance myself from my statements (which are actually his). The man and the woman at the back of the shop are conducting a whispered conversation which I fortunately can't hear. The white-haired woman behind the counter pushes the half-wrapped book aside and asks, 'Would you like a cup of coffee?' I can tell how seedy I look from her expression.

Fortunately she ignores my identical return question. Perhaps she understands what is wrong with me. (This is worse than it was. Then I could make myself more or less understood with the help of approximate sentences, proverbs and synonyms. Now I'm the prisoner of other people's language!)

Richard Fielemieg doesn't understand in any case. I now remember exactly who he is. In the past, when I did my own selling, I was often in his shop. He was the most stubborn bookseller I have ever met. He had an opinion on every book, no publisher was any good. If you were to believe Fielemieg the whole industry was doomed. But when it came to ordering he never took more than a few pathetic single copies and at the last moment even tried to negotiate a higher discount.

I turn away from him in order to reduce the chance of a conversation and walk across to a table full of books. One I recognize immediately. I pick up the book in its wine-red jacket. Herman Poelgeest, *The Uninhabited Island*. I turn to the title page. At the bottom is the name of the publisher: Discus. In fact I'd expected something else, a written dedication from Herman. I don't know why. I leaf through the book, recognize the typeface: Bembo. Then I turn to the last paragraph.

'Each time he completed the circuit of the beach, he saw new tracks in the sand, footprints of yet another new creature which he tirelessly set out in search of in the hope of finding it this time. He no longer looked out across the sea, where the sails of passing ships on the horizon had long been replaced by smoking funnels.'

Richard Fielemieg comes over and stands next to me. I hurriedly replace the book on the pile.

The woman with white hair calls behind my back, 'Your coffee!'

'Your coffee,' I say to the bookseller.

'No, yours,' he says politely and rather anxiously.

'No, yours,' I retort.

The bookseller looks past me. He has thin, lank hair and protruding ears. He acts as though this conversation hasn't taken place and starts talking about the book I had in my hand just now.

'Of course it's not as good as Tournier's adaptation of the same theme, but the idea of Man Friday being a hallucination of Crusoe's is very original. We're selling a lot at the moment.'

He looks at me expectantly. He has spoken so quickly that the mechanism which is forcing me to repeat can't handle it. It allows me to be silent.

'Your coffee,' he says, pointing to the three cups on the counter where the white-haired woman has meanwhile wrapped the book and handed it to the man and the woman.

'Good afternoon,' says the man, who has put on a pair of sunglasses.

'Good afternoon,' says my voice loudly. The man and the woman hurry out of the shop. I follow them. When they see me coming out, they start running. I shake my head, laugh and walk casually out to my bike across the road.

Fielemieg stands in the doorway of his shop. The white-haired woman stands behind him slightly to one side and rests both her hands on his right shoulder. They watch as I get on the bike and ride off. I moisten my lips, and feel the cool wind passing over them.

Again I see a blue signpost with white lettering. Yes, I still want to go to the mountains. Thinner air helps you think better. I follow the instructions and turn right. According to the signpost to 'Bergen aan Zee' the mountains are by the sea, as they often are.

The fir trees in the lane I'm now cycling along bend over the road, their crowns touching. Lines of cars with strange number plates come to meet me. I can't connect this fact with what I have just observed. The geography of my life seems quite confused. For example I can't imagine that I am abroad. How could I have found Fielemieg's bookshop there? And the customers in the bookshop were speaking Dutch anyway.

At the end of the shady lane the wooded countryside suddenly slopes upwards. The foot of the mountains! So the sea can't be far either. I stand on the pedals and start the climb. Above my head I can hear the seagulls calling invitingly. The sun is still between the trees. When the path makes a sharp right-hand turn I am completely dazzled for a moment. When I can see again the mountains have disappeared, as though they were a piece of scenery abruptly pulled away, and I ride into an undulating landscape of dunes. On the road next to me is a queue of cars with fuming exhausts. I have to keep well to the right; on the cycle path cyclists in summer clothes are coming towards me in long lines. Horns and bells are sounded loudly. Fists are raised. It's as if these people are fleeing the scene of some catastrophe.

Dotting the pale marram grass growing on the slopes of the dunes there are dusty green bushes with bright red berries, shining like beads. I would like to linger there (I am happy with this old-fashioned sentence, which derives from a distant past or a book), but the dunes are closed off from the road on both sides by barbed wire.

I must have misinterpreted the words on the signpost. Suddenly it occurs to me that this might be a place name and not a description. Place names which seem just to be there and which the landscape doesn't necessarily conform to.

Then the road drops sharply downwards and I rush at top speed into a chaotic built-up area of scattered houses and occasional blocks of flats. I flash past a little church and a car park in which gaps are gradually appearing, past a terrace of postwar houses with flat roofs, their front gardens full of stacked plastic garden furniture. Everywhere colourful swimsuits hang out to dry on washing lines.

The road ends in a large square. I brake, get off the bike and try to cross between the solid line of crawling cars to the other side where there is a smaller square surrounded by snack bars and cafés. The square is littered with empty paper bags and plastic chip trays. A stream of people, often with whining children and barking and jumping dogs in tow comes towards me. Behind them I can already see the calm, glistening sea below, as if it's trying to say: you can rely on me, when you've seen the word 'sea' you can be sure I'm not far away.

I put the bike against a wall and lock it, and walk past a caravan converted into a shop selling filled rolls. On a blackboard at the front it says in large white letters: 'We serve excellent rolls'.

Many children coming from the beach are wearing coloured T-shirts with all kinds of writing on them, mainly in English. Most are speaking German. Most of the words bear no relationship at all to the wearers. A fat woman is shrouded in a pink landscape full of sickly green palm trees under which is the name of the place depicted in black letters, the island of Hawaii. A thin boy in a white T-shirt proclaims, 'I am here', a sentence which for once doesn't stretch the truth, but for that very reason seems a little superfluous.

I can tell from their contented faces that the words and text surrounding them don't disconcert all these people coming back from the beach in the least, that they may not even notice them, let alone compare the text with reality. I also think that that's normal and that I too ought to make a division between words and the world, but I still can't do it automatically. I'm continually struck by new examples of inaccuracy on signs or shops. 'Hot sausages today' it says on the front of a closed café. 'We never close', says a sign placed against a delivery bike with an arrow on it pointing in the direction of the sea.

The square slopes downwards and turns into a path down to the beach made of wooden duckboarding. I focus my eyes on the letterless sea and walk on to the beach.

The tide is in. The water's foaming edge slowly creeps on to the land, filling up the large and small footprints in the sand. Sandcastles crumble in the advancing water. A line of gulls bobs just behind the surf like a convoy awaiting orders. The sun hanging just above the horizon casts a strip of orange ripples over the water.

I walk slowly along the high-tide mark and feel myself coming to rest, the language in my head subsiding and myself just a body with a consciousness which has no wish to extend any further than its presence here, walking along this beach.

The further away I go from the way down, the quieter it gets on the beach. The edge of the dunes breaks off abruptly here. The undulating patterns of the waves from last year's autumn storms are still clearly visible in the layers of sand. These are signs, stories too, but they need no words.

I stop at one of the bulging iron rubbish bins. I look among the paper, tubs and dented beer cans for something edible. I pull a half full bag of chips out from under an empty plastic bottle. I sit on the ground with the bag, trying to rest my back against the bin.

A group of boys approaches me. One of them has a burning torch in his hand. Further down the beach I can see the rubbish bins burning. I stay calmly where I am and stuff the cold, tough sticks of fried potato into my mouth one by one.

When the boys come close they form a circle round me. A dark lad with a white scar on his right cheek says, 'Nice chips, grandad?'

The copying machine I've obviously become repeats his question.

The boy takes a couple of steps forward. He looks into the chip bag in my hand. 'Christ almighty,' he says. 'Do you eat out of rubbish bins?'

My reply is his question.

He grabs me by my collar and shakes me back and forth. The bag falls out of my hand into the sand.

'Do you think you're a comic?' he shouts, his voice breaking. And again I can do nothing but pay him back in the same coin. I try to pull myself free.

One of the boys shouts, 'Leave him be, Johan, you can see the bloke's nuts.'

The dark boy lets me go. I fall back with a bang against the rubbish bin, which suddenly catches fire above my head.

It's as though fear of the flames in the heat of the fire above my head releases words in me. I jump up. The boys shrink back in a bunch.

'You load of bastards,' I hear from my mouth, full of anger and conviction.

'Old fart,' one of them shouts. 'Stinking poof, tramp,' screams another.

The spell is broken. I no longer dance to the tune of other people's words. A hoarse roar rises from my throat. I advance on them with clenched fists.

'I'm going to drown you one by one,' I scream. 'I'm going to hold your heads under water until you can't say another word.'

'*Schweinhund*,' shouts a golden-haired boy. But my language now has the upper hand. They slowly retreat.

'You're full of shit,' I shout after them. 'You can get stuffed, you can all get stuffed.'

I'm no longer swearing, but am in a free improvisation which finally makes me burst into wordless song. But the boys have long ago stopped listening. They've turned and are running away passing an imaginary ball from one to another.

I turn to the almost motionless expanse of water behind which the sun has disappeared like an orange ball, pulling its colours behind it. For a moment it holds the silhouette of a sailing boat in its halo of light, and then the final curve disappears below the horizon.

I undress and walk into the sea. My body recognizes the situation immediately. I slowly sink forward into the water and swim off. I want to go to meet the trembling cone of light which is becoming shorter and shorter. Nevertheless after about ten strokes my body turns and swims back to where I can stand again. I wash myself with the salt water until I feel that all the dirt is off my skin. Then I walk back towards the beach, pick my clothes up and wash them in the surf. I wring them out as well as I can.

I am now completely alone. The boys have set fire to all the rubbish bins on their route. There's nothing more to eat anywhere. Plastic bottles and ice lolly sticks smoulder in the smoking, stinking bins. When I spot a way up through the dunes, I start climbing.

I turn round one last time, holding my wet clothes in one hand, my shoes in the other. The evening seems to be climbing out of the sea, searching for a path into the sky strewn with stars. However dangerous water can sometimes be, it now surrenders itself, lapping gently, to the silent beach.

'Sea,' I say, and again, 'sea', and I realize how the water and the word slip into each other like a hand into a glove. I turn round and walk in the direction of the hills, still glowing in the dark and retaining the warmth of the day in their pale grass. To my amazement I feel an erection coming on.

Not a breath of wind around me; not a leaf, not a bush stirs. Now and again I hear a slight rustling in the grass to the side. The moon is almost full. I still see the moon with a face, a childhood habit I've never been able to shake off. The moonlight descends almost shyly on the dunes. The blurred outline of my long shadow falls across the sand dune I'm climbing. The clothes are hanging heavily over my left arm. It seems so normal to walk along naked, that I have the urge to drop them, leave everything behind.

I imagine a meeting with a woman. The woman is naked like me. I clearly see the loosely hanging blond hair moving backwards and forwards across her shoulder blades as she comes towards me, hips swaying.

When she is close to me I recognize her. I take her into a dip in the dunes, spread out my clothes and lie down on my back in the sand next to them.

'Marion,' I whisper, lending her my hand, 'Marion,' and feel how greedily my sex is trembling and throbbing in her hand and the wave mounts in my loins and then bursts out and floods over me.

Slowly the body's dominance recedes and Marion's face appears to me, narrow and shy, as I first knew it in the invoicing department at Orion Publishers, where I started in the business as a lad of twenty-three. The body seems to retreat further and further. Universal life, dictated by physical processes over which I have no control, gives way to personal, clearly defined memories, which must have been trying in vain to gain admittance all this time. 'Marion,' I whisper.

She is standing in our conservatory watering the plants with the red plastic watering can that Wouter used to play with in the bath. I lift my son out of the water. I try to dry him, but he grabs the towel from my hands. He wants to do it himself, perhaps he's embarrassed at standing there naked like that in front of his father. Marion smiles. The other day I caught him in the bath; he was sitting playing with himself. Her teeth protrude a little when she laughs, and then I call her Bunny and she calls me Slant Eyes. Words that I now whisper softly to myself in the dunes, words that have been restored to me, the first building blocks of a life which seemed lost for ever.

Exactly how long have I been away? Perhaps I've already been reported missing. They must have been looking for me. What did they think at the publishers when I didn't show up? But again: for how long?

I try to think about it, remember what might have happened, but there's nothing, no image at all. An empty mirror. My memory can't have been functioning. I shiver at the idea that I have been living all this time on a kind of automatic pilot.

I'm somewhere on the coast. Tomorrow I must ring Marion, when it's light and the shops are open. And again I see her standing in the conservatory with her back to me. Looking worried, she pushes back the net curtains and scans the avenue in front of her house. 238407. That's the number I must dial to get through to her, to hear her say in her light, confident voice: 'Marion Zomer speaking.'

I look up at the galaxies fanning out above my head. Between them desolate black sections of apparent nothingness.

I should like to sleep (or I may have been asleep). Whenever I try to remember anything from the last few days there is nothing but a bright shadowless space. Emotionally no time has passed, there has been no time at all, although that is basically inconceivable. Things must have happened, I must have eaten and slept. I feel as an animal must feel, alone in space, moving from nothing to nowhere. But what happened immediately before the 'incident', as I now call it for want of a better word, I can remember exactly.

I was driving over to to see Karel van de Oever, a former salesman of ours whose seventieth birthday it was. There was a bunch of flowers for his wife on the back seat. In the glove compartment there was a bound and signed copy of *The Uninhabited Island* by Herman Poelgeest, which had just come out. I had high hopes of that novel and I knew that Van de Oever, who had sold a lot of Poelgeest's work, would be honoured with a personal dedication from the writer. But then? Then nothing else. Then? The road, the car, myself all stopped until I found myself again here, naked in a dip in the dunes.

The night stays sultry. Sometimes high above me I hear the sound of an airliner flying in over the sea. The occasional bird flaps its wings in a tree. The motionless sand has arranged itself under my body. I pick a stalk of grass and chew on it. Hunger makes my empty stomach rumble.

Yet I must have been eating all that time. But how long was 'all that time'? Or did someone feed me? I can't remember anyone, just as I can't remember any place that I've been, must have been.

I'm longing for home, for a bed, for Marion, who will put on a Beethoven string quartet for me while I sit down at my desk in the front room to start on a new manuscript. What have Peter, Ankie and Rob been doing all that time? There's that phrase again, which makes me slightly desperate, 'all that time'.

When there's no time you're lost in empty space. And yet I can't remember being frightened or unhappy. Nonexistence? But no one can imagine such a thing. As long as you're alive you're *there*. Your body proves that to you, although it refuses to surrender the memory of it and gives you another instead.

I must have been about twelve. Without telling anyone of my plans I had gone skating one Saturday morning along the ditches beyond the village. Other children skated there but I had dreamt up the plan of going on an expedition. I had hidden a map of the province under my clothes. I had stolen a two-and-a-half guilder coin from my mother's purse to be able to buy some food, which I called provisions, on the way. Via the narrow ditches with their bumpy ice I reached the canals and lakes where I soon met no one else. The only sound was made by the sweeping blades of my skates. That sound seemed to be accompanied by a faint echo beneath the ice's black shiny surface. Then I fell through. As suddenly as that, without transition from the hard surface into the icy water of the hole. I must have panicked for a moment, then my body took over from me, turned me round and struggled towards the black spot which showed me the hole in the ice. I scrambled towards the edge and I was able to clamber ashore without the sides crumbling. I took off my skates and began running over the lightly frosted meadows in the direction of the village. I had to keep jogging, although that got more and more difficult. My slowly freezing clothes felt heavier and heavier, closing round me like a stiff suit of armour. When I finally stumbled into the kitchen gasping and crying, my father, a steaming cup of coffee in his hand, asked where I had left my skates. I don't know, I stammered. But of course I did know. I had thrown them into the hole in fear and rage where they had kept floating for a moment before disappearing into the depths, dragging a long stream of skate bindings behind them.

It slowly starts to get light. The bright sunlight drives back the moon, the stars, except for an occasional pale planet, have retreated, the sky is the colour of dark ink and starting from below will soon regain its familiar blue tinge. The clothes beside me are still wet, but at least they no longer stink. Hoisting myself into my rough clothes I can feel that my hair is full of salt. Then I set out on my way back.

Six

I have returned to my life, my head is again full of information I can use, with which I should be able to find the way back home.

A man in a dark blue tracksuit edged with white trots past me and calls 'Tschüss'. A German, like so many Germans who stay on the coast in the summer. Once I'm on the beach, I may be able to get my bearings better than in this undulating dune landscape accented here and there with dark clumps of fir trees allowing the gentle breeze to rustle through their tops. I follow the German's fresh tracks, the deep imprint of his large trainers in the soft sand.

When I have climbed another gentle hill, I see a number of villas scattered along the edge of a dune. The sea must be somewhere there. I change direction, no longer following the German's tracks, and climb through dips in the dunes, walk over crackling dead twigs and through the tough, hard marram grass which pricks my calves.

I find my way to a brick road. A little later I find a signpost with a name on it and I know where I am: Bergen aan Zee. Less than thirty miles from home! I walk along the road, past a tall, gloomy building glassed in along the whole of its front, in which old people sit silently at long benches with white cups of coffee. On a piece of waste ground a man is flying a red kite for his little son. The kite bobs up and down in the weak thermal current; for a moment it seems to be about to dive to earth with a wild rattle, but then a passing ground wind lifts it and sends it straight up to its zenith. I see the reel spinning round between the man's outstretched hands and watch the bright red kite up there as it makes the invisible motions of the wind visible and dances in the sky.

The houses I saw just now from the dunes are right in front of me. A mustard-yellow country bus without passengers circles a roundabout and disappears from view round the corner of one of the houses.

The villagers seem still to be asleep. There are boards in windows everywhere. *Zimmer. Frühstück.* I pass a hotel called 'Sun All Around'. On a closed herring stall there is a picture of some glassy-looking fish making their way towards the sea along the shiny brown-painted planks.

Then I see a square that I recognize immediately. I once rented an apartment there with Marion and Wouter in the concrete block of flats that closes off the square from the dunes on the eastern side. There is no sign of life yet either, in the rooms of the downstairs flats, full of wicker furniture and carelessly discarded holiday clothes.

The shops and snack bars on the narrow square next to the Van Wijckplein are closed. I walk in the direction of the path down to the beach. A sign low down on a trailer announces: 'We make excellent rolls', but the counter is closed by two white shutters. What's more, I have no money to buy anything to eat.

I go down to the beach over the wooden duckboarding. The tide is out. The sunlight seems to be bobbing above the sea mist. A black dog is scratching about along the tide-line, and shoots off when it sees me. It's nice to feel the hard wet sand under my shoes. There are no footprints in the untouched, newly formed layer of sand. When I look back my own footprints are the only ones among the white and blue-black shells.

A little further on a terrace café has put out its white chairs but the beach pavilion beyond, with its yellow Nutricia Dairy Drink flag, is still closed. I will wait there until the village wakes up and people appear on the beach. Then I can phone Marion and tell her to come and get me.

In the distance I hear a car engine. When I look in the direction of the sound, I see a jeep heading fast towards me along the shoreline. Seagulls stand in a straight line along the edge of the surf and rise with a slow flapping of wings when the jeep approaches.

When the car is a few hundred yards from me, it swerves across the beach in my direction. There are two policemen in the jeep. It stops in an elegant arc in front of the beach pavilion. One of the policemen climbs out and comes towards me. I get up from the plastic seat.

'Good morning,' says the young man, touching his cap politely. A thin moustache runs under his sharp nose like a shoelace.

'Good morning,' I reply.

'Could I ask you something,' says the young man, leafing through a notebook he has produced from the breast pocket of his uniform.

'Of course,' I say. 'Go right ahead.'

'Might you be Mr Zomer? Kees Zomer?'

'That's right,' I say. 'But how do you know that?'

'You were reported missing more than a week ago. Yesterday somebody who knew you identified you in Bergen. We've been looking for you since then.'

'Strange,' I say. 'I can't remember having been away for so long, or being in Bergen at all.'

'Would you mind coming with us,' says the policeman.

I nod. I can phone Marion from the police station.

The driver of the jeep seems rather older than the policeman with the moustache. He just nods briefly when the young policeman informs him of my identity. He accelerates too hard so that the front wheels spin in the sand for a moment. Then he jerks the front wheels to the left and drives the jeep more slowly on to the hard sand. The wind sweeps through my shirt, which is still damp. I shiver. The young policeman looks at me quizzically over his shoulder, but says nothing. I look at the sea, at the sun which has now extricated itself from the veils of mist. Now and then we pass people, mostly accompanied by a dog.

'It's threatening to be a nice day,' says the young policeman.

'Sunday,' says the older one.

Sunday. That explains the abandoned look of the village.

The jeep now turns towards the dunes up an exit from the beach, bumping over the iron sheets which have been laid there until the wheels get a grip on the cobbles of the promenade. We turn on to the Zeeweg in the direction of Bergen.

'Who was it saw me in Bergen?' I ask the young policeman.

'Fielemieg, from the bookshop,' he replies.

'We'll ask the questions at the station,' says the older policeman, correcting him.

There is a moment's silence. Two magpies flutter low over the Eeuwigelaan into the woods.

130

'Strange,' I say. 'I don't remember seeing him.'

'See without being seen,' says the young policeman joking. 'That's what our sergeant in the army always used to say. See without being seen. Military Handbook, page such and such.'

The jeep stops in the car park in front of a square stone building. Through the windows I see that there are neon lights on in the ceiling. The young policeman holds open the dark blue front door. I step into a corridor with tiles up to waist height. The young policeman points to a wooden bench against the wall.

'Have a seat. Sergeant Scholten will be with you in just a moment.'

I smile. This is the first time in my life I've had dealings with the police.

On the wall opposite me, above the white-tiled wall, is a map of North Holland. I get up and walk towards it. My finger follows the route from Bergen aan Zee to Heemstede, and then draws a wide arc around the area where I must have been wandering. I read the names of villages and hamlets, but none of them evokes memories of a recent visit. Then a door opens at the end of the corridor. A corpulent man of my own age, with a blue shirt taut across his belly, comes towards me with an outstretched hand.

Sergeant Scholten points to a chair in front of a simple steel desk on which there are some folders and a tin sandwich box displaying its contents. The policeman walks over to the window and pulls down the blinds. Then he sits down opposite me. I can't take my eyes off the sandwiches in the tin and imagine that the man opposite must hear my stomach rumbling clearly. He rubs his broad hands and watches the two flies on the ceiling for a moment. Then he fixes me with a friendly, enquiring gaze.

'Tell me about it,' he says, taking a piece of paper out of one of the folders and producing a ballpoint pen from the breast pocket of his shirt.

'I don't know,' I say. 'There isn't much to tell.'

'What do you mean?'

'I can't remember how I got here. How I've been living all this time.'

Sergeant Scholten writes something down. Now he hears the rumbling of my stomach. He looks up in surprise from the paper and then, still writing, pushes the sandwich box in my direction.

'Go right ahead,' he says. 'Jam and cheese. We've nothing else in stock.'

He puts down his pen and gets up. 'I'll go and get some coffee. How do you like it?'

'Milk and sugar, please,' I say, taking the top sandwich from the tin, a cheese sandwich that tastes of jam too. But I'm too hungry to be finicky.

Once the sergeant has left the room I get up and walk around the desk. The policeman has written only one word on the paper. Blackout. And after it a question mark. One word to explain my absence. It's an almost pathetic sight. A policeman is out to form an impression of the true course of events on the basis of all kinds of disparate information, a story with a causal connection, first this, then that. A reconstruction. But in my case there was no trail to follow. That one word on the otherwise empty paper expressed impotence, the question mark suspicion.

I hear his footsteps approaching down the corridor and quickly sit back in my seat. The sergeant puts a thick earthenware mug down in front of me.

'It's from early this morning,' he says by way of excuse. He sits down and stares at the word on the paper for a moment.

He doesn't really know how to continue the conversation.

When my mouth is empty, I say, pointing to a telephone, 'Might I ring my wife?'

'We've done it already,' says the sergeant. 'Your wife is on her way.' He has brown, roundish eyes, which regard me sympathetically for a moment, but then again assume the observant look of a policeman on duty.

'Your wife,' he says. 'You know your wife's name?'

'Of course I know my wife's name,' I say in irritation. 'Marion Zomer. My address is Langevoortlaan 12 in Heemstede and my telephone number is 238407.'

The sergeant takes the top folder off the pile and opens it. He nods in approval without looking at me.

'You don't understand,' I say. 'The only thing that I can't remember are the days that I have been missing. Apart from that I know everything. I must have had a kind of blackout.'

I look straight at the sergeant. He rubs the broad bridge of his nose with two fingers of his left hand.

'It says here, in your wife's statement, that you left the house at a quarter past four on the afternoon of Wednesday 2 August, in a Peugeot 203, registration number DJ-34-ST, year of manufacture 1986. You were going to see an ex-colleague, Karel van de Oever, in Koog aan de Zaan, who was having his seventieth birthday that day.'

I nod. 'That's right. In the glove compartment there was a copy of a book by one of my authors with a special dedication to Karel in it.'

The sergeant leans back in his office chair and folds his hands, unadorned except for a thick wedding ring.

'But the strange thing is that that car of yours has disappeared without trace. Don't you think that's odd?'

I look at him. What can I say?

'Tell me. Can you remember an accident? Did you suddenly feel ill for a moment and come off the road?'

I shake my head despondently and swallow some of the lukewarm coffee.

'I don't know,' I say helplessly. 'I really don't.'

'But you do remember getting into the car?'

'Yes,' I say, 'I remember that. I took the A9, towards Alkmaar.'

Sergeant Scholten writes. 'Do you remember going through the Velsen Tunnel?'

'That too.'

'Do you remember what exits you passed after that?'

'I didn't pay special attention.'

'Try to remember. It'll be of the greatest importance in helping us trace the vehicle.'

'I understand,' I say.

'Beverwijk, Castricum, Akersloot. Do any of those names ring a bell?'

I shake my head. 'I think it's awful too,' I say. 'You must understand how awful it is not to be able to remember a thing, though you've gone on living all that time.'

Scholten looks in the folder again. 'It says here that your wife contacted the police on Monday 7 August. Your description was broadcast on Wednesday, but no one had seen you in all that time. Until you appeared on the bike here in Bergen at Fielemieg's bookshop on 12 August. Fielemieg knew about your disappearance and immediately rang us. He said on that occasion – and I quote, "Mister Zomer made a harassed and rather confused impression. He didn't seem to be able to follow the conversation we were having and simply repeated all questions which were put to him instead of giving an intelligible answer." '

'I'm sure that's true,' I say, 'but I can't remember anything about it.'

'You do know Mr Fielemieg, don't you?'

'Of course. From long ago. When I was a publisher's rep myself.'

Scholten opens the folder in front of him and adds the sheet of paper on which he has been making notes. 'Well,' he says, 'then I don't know what else to say either. We'll list the car as missing for the time being. Missing's better than disappeared. Disappeared can't be put in a report. It's possible of course, but I prefer not to.'

'I understand,' I say.

The sergeant picks up the folder and gets up. 'I'm going to close this file. You can stay here and wait for your wife. She'll be here any minute.'

He shakes hands with me and gives me a last searching look. 'If I were you I'd consult a doctor as soon as possible,' he says.

I nod and look straight ahead until I hear the door close behind me. Then I take the jam sandwich from the tin too.

As I chew I look around. At the back of the room is a tall steel filing cabinet, next to it a wooden coatstand with nothing but a belt on it. In the left-hand corner of the room is a small TV on a black table.

I get up and walk over to the television. There is a programme guide on the set. I have no idea what has happened in the world since my departure. My hand moves towards the button. No, it's better to wait for Marion, to let her fill the hole in my memory and not newsreaders and commentators.

I take the guide with me to my chair at the desk and start leafing through it. It's last week's. These programmes were broadcast in the period that I had a consciousness but no memory linked to it. Perhaps that's why I read the descriptions so avidly. As though I'm trying to fill the emptiness of that week with external events.

'Young doctor Dmitri Malyanov does field work in the deserts of Turkmenistan. He is trying to prove that there is a relationship between health and morality, between (low) infant mortality rates and religious experience. Woman makes an abortion decision dependent on the death or survival of her husband. Margo runs away from home. Her mother says that she need not come back, but her father misses her terribly. Is a foster-family the right thing for her? A museum attendant explains why the trifling objects in his museum are important. The search for old friends who have vanished without trace. Will the abolition of agricultural subsidies in Eastern Europe cause food prices to rise? The rapid changes of the 1960s caused four million Japanese to move from the countryside to the cities to work in the new factories. At the same time the campaign for birth control got under way.'

All these stories, all these summaries and explanations are almost too much for me, though as I read I am seized by a joy which at first I don't understand. I read on with childish delight.

'Woman journalist does a lot for a good story on the office. Wife of quiet architect murdered, his daughter raped. When police make no headway, the frenzied architect launches single-handed campaign of vengeance.'

Right. Yes, that's how life should be! And I want to be part of that life again, to be caught up in the roaring merry-go-round in which one event leads to another. Real or fictitious, it doesn't matter. It's stories that keep people going. I can't remember exactly what has happened to me in the time that has just passed, but one thing I know for sure: I was living in a space where there were no more stories, as if under a glass bell jar from which the air had been extracted.

Sergeant Scholten wouldn't have understood anything like that. A space without stories is something a policeman would prefer not to exist. Once I'm home I'll have my fill of stories, until I have the feeling again that like everyone else, I am full of the life that drags us from one event to the next.

The door opens. I turn my head towards the doorway and feel my eyes fill with tears.

Marion kneels beside me, takes my head in her hands.

'I'm so ashamed,' I sob. 'I'm ashamed I've been away without knowing where.'

My hands feel all over her body as though they can't believe it is her, Marion, in the flesh. She pushes me gently but firmly away. Stroking my head with one hand, she gets up and takes mine in the other.

'Come on,' she says. I get up, holding her hand like a small child. In the doorway stands Sergeant Scholten with a large gleaming forehead.

'So that's solved,' he said. In the corridor he shakes both our hands earnestly and at length, as though solemnizing a marriage.

'Safe journey home,' he calls after us from the open door of the police station. He's a village policeman, used to small problems. He'll certainly be glad to be rid of this tricky case.

Seven

Outside Marion puts an arm around me and hugs me tightly for a moment.

'We've been so worried,' she says, taking the car keys out of her leather windcheater with her free hand. Only when she has let go of me and walks round the Panda, do I take in the full picture of her living presence. Under the open jacket she is wearing a thin beige sweater over white cotton trousers. She has on brown moccasins. She leans on the roof of the car with both hands.

'What are you looking at? Come on, get in.'

Again I feel my eyes filling with tears. 'You're so familiar to me,' I mutter. 'I feel so much better now I can see you right in front of me.'

She gently strokes my nose, my lips, my cheeks with a forefinger, as though trying to imprint my face on her mind like a blind person. I stare straight ahead through the windscreen. Then she puts the key in the ignition. She looks at me.

'Is something wrong?'

I shake my head. For a second I felt as if I no longer knew which side was left and which right, what was ahead and what was behind; but now I'm nestling in the seat next to her and following the direction the car is taking. We're going home.

'We've been so worried,' she repeats.

'How's Wouter?'

'Fine. He had a hockey match. And anyway I thought it would be better if he didn't come with me. After all, I didn't know what state I'd find you in. How do you feel, Kees?'

'Thawed out,' I say. 'Something like that. Although that's more of an image than what actually happened. I don't know what happened to me.'

'And the car?'

'No idea. I know I got into it, that I was on my way to see Karel. And then nothing. Then there's a complete full stop in my head.'

'It'll come back,' she says.

I look sideways at her. There are three wrinkles between her frowning eyebrows. She always drives with a frown, and when she drives underneath a bridge or a viaduct she always ducks, almost imperceptibly, bless her.

'I love you so much,' I whisper.

'Don't,' she says. 'I'm driving. Later.'

I look out at the fields, the ditches between them. The sun is reflected harshly in a couple of panes of glass from a complex of greenhouses in the distance.

'It all seems so familiar,' I say. 'But it's the memory of the past, not of the period I've just been through.'

'Don't think about it,' she says.

'I can't think about it,' I say. 'When there's been nothing there. There's only that feeling.'

'What feeling?'

'A kind of threat. As though I can simply fall through a hole at any moment.'

We now turn on to the Alkmaar ring road. There aren't many cars about; I remember that it's Sunday morning.

'As though something in me doesn't quite want to

believe what I see. Reality should be something you take for granted, but I can't.'

'Not yet. It'll come back.'

The sun glints on the open water of Alkmaar Lake, across which a couple of sailing boats with white sails seem to be making scarcely any progress.

'I love it here,' says Marion, 'with all those straight lines of trees across the countryside.'

'Windbreaks,' I say.

'Oh,' she says, 'is that what you call them?'

'It's a word from the past,' I say. 'At least that's what it feels like. Windbreaks. I can still hear Dad calling them that.'

One of the few clouds half obscures the sun, creating a searchlight beam which casts a line of rays across the sparkling water.

'On a lake like this I once fell through the ice in winter. I had to go back the following day because I had left my skates behind. But there was no sign of the hole. It had frozen over completely. There was a thin dusting of snow over the top. I knew the place exactly, but Dad, who had come with me, looked at the smooth white surface in disbelief. I pointed to the spot and felt as if I was lying to him, but I knew for certain that there under the black ice, at the bottom of the canal, were my skates.'

Marion says nothing. She pushes the button of the car radio. I recognize the piano music immediately.

'Haydn,' I say. 'That must be Haydn.'

'Do you love it so much?' she asks when she sees tears running involuntarily down my cheeks.

'It's the only consolation,' I say hoarsely. 'Music pulls you through the worst misery.'

'This sounds pretty cheerful, though,' she says.

'We've got it at home,' I say.

'Only another five miles,' she says, 'and we'll be there.'

I listen to the slow movement of the sonata. Wooden signs appear in the fields, advertising sherry and water beds. A cigar with a gold label floats on a large red hoarding. 'Out of puff?' it says in white lettering underneath. I recognize the pun, the reference to a past slogan, but it irritates me. Once I start paying attention, the approaching built-up area is heralded by a chorus of puns and slogans. 'Keep the sun out', it says on the roof of a factory building where sunblinds are obviously manufactured. 'Be quick about it', says a young girl in a tight-fitting black body stocking, pointing to a bilious green sports car with wire wheels. I read the signs which are out of place in the landscape, polluting the last green fields with their words. A sleek brown horse stands with its head resting on a gate looking at an area of ground on to which sand slurry has been pumped and allowed to dry.

Building materials and loose beams lie in piles around sheet-iron sheds. Through the windows of low brick buildings I see rows of empty desks. A lorry with a trailer turns slowly on to the motorway from a factory site. The buildings and factories on the industrial estate on either side of the road are separate from each other, self-contained, absorbed in production. Situated next to each other, on roads and turn-offs, they imitate a city with no centre, no heart. Everyone for themselves. Together with their products they will one day disappear, leaving nothing behind except a bare plain. No, this landscape has no continuity at all. People exist there without looking at it, their hands perform the necessary actions until they can go home again, back to the protection and order of their interiors.

And high above this chaotic built-up area the wires of electricity pylons continue like a musical stave in the direction of the town, the compact blocks of flats on the horizon. Only the light holds this view together. No coherence at all. It astonishes me that people can't see this, that everyone obviously regards this landscape as perfectly natural.

The pianist begins the fast final movement of the sonata. Marion whistles along with the constantly recurring theme. Sloping walls of corrugated iron sheeting now rise on both sides of the motorway. A sign with an arrow pointing to the right. 'Hazardous substances'. A little later we enter a tunnel. My body stiffens. I look sideways. Marion has put on her headlights and, sure enough, she is cringing slightly. The whole landscape has disappeared for a while and the music can no longer penetrate the concrete which carries the water of the North Sea Canal above us. The end of the tunnel comes towards me. Then the music again swirls into the car in wild ecstatic arpeggios.

'Wonderful,' says Marion when the music has finished. She turns off the radio.

The fields, the trees and the ditches have finally given way to rows of flats, sometimes interspersed with low-rise houses of an earlier date. The number of words, signs and shop windows increases. People stand talking on a mown expanse of grass between two blocks of flats. They seem completely at ease. Nothing in their behaviour indicates that they are aware of their surroundings.

'Astonishing,' I say.

'What?'

'That all those people behave like that, seem to be

so immune to all those captions and messages around them.'

'They live here. Eventually you stop seeing it.'

'That's what I mean. The fact that they feel at home here.'

For a moment I have the feeling that we are driving into the Langevoortlaan from the wrong direction, that the small red-brick villa should be on the other side of the road. Then the inner picture again merges with the outer one.

'We're here,' says Marion.

In the conservatory there are the familiar fatsia and the ornamental palm with its narrow fanning leaves. When we get out I can see the neighbours on the left standing side by side in their bay windows to the left and to the right. An old man and an old woman with grey hair. They wave. I recognize them, but they refuse to become real. The moment they drop their hands they again assume the pose of mannequins.

I follow Marion cautiously up the paved garden path. I'm glad I know the name of the shrub in the right-hand corner of the garden. Rhododendron. A wonderful word like that gives your eyes something to hold on to. I can't understand where that emotion keeps welling up from.

When Marion opens the front door I inhale loudly, taking in the smell of the house.

'It's like coming back from holiday, isn't it,' says Marion. 'That feeling.'

I nod, but that is not what it's like. The smell is completely unfamiliar. Not unpleasant, but unknown.

'Yes,' I say. 'That always used to surprise me. That you only smelled the smell when you'd been away for a while. Otherwise never at all.'

143

When I walk down the hall to the living room, I feel I am taking up my past where I left off. The room is the room I have always known, but the recognition seems not to come from inside but is like a sort of photo caption. Or like that game of Electro. I stop in the middle of the room, take in the overcrowded bookcase, the empty white desk at the back, the canvas-covered sofa and the table with four straight-backed chairs, as I would look at a furniture catalogue.

'What are you thinking about?' Marion puts her arms round me. I can feel her soft blond hair rubbing my cheek.

'It's weird,' I say. 'I can't remember anything about the recent past. But occasionally something suddenly surfaces from long ago. Can you remember that we bought an Electro game for Wouter?'

'Vaguely. It must have been at least ten years ago.'

'I can see it so clearly in front of me. There were cards with words on which you had to put under the matching picture. "Key" by key. "Scooter" by the picture of a scooter. Then there were two wires with plugs on which you had to put into the holes in the case. If the combination of word and picture was right, a light lit up in the box, a red light.'

'But what are you getting at?' she says hesitantly, and walks towards the conservatory. I follow her and sit down in one of the wicker chairs which have been sprayed navy blue.

'I know I'm talking in images. But I can't help it. That's how it was. I couldn't make contact any more. Things were around me, I knew their names, but what was in between, the bridge, was missing.'

Marion sits down opposite me and looks at me with her pale blue eyes. She is so eager to understand me, but

I know she can't. So I stroke her hand gently. 'It can't be understood,' I say consolingly.

Head bent, she shakes her hair back and forth in front of her face.

'Don't do that,' I say. 'I want to keep looking at your face.'

'I'm here,' she says and smiles at me through a curtain of hair. She gets up and says she's going to put on some coffee.

I get up too, intending to follow her, but then stop by the record player built into the bookcase. I look among the records until I've found the box set of Haydn piano sonatas. I take out a record and put it on. I press the button of the amplifier as if it were the most natural thing in the world. Actions that produce a result: a soft hissing sound like an old radio, and then suddenly the limpid piano music fills the room. I dance a couple of steps in time with the music. My body accepts me completely. Swaying, I look around me. I can't shake off the feeling of being a guest here.

Marion comes back with the coffee: that is, to my indescribable joy she enters the room with a white tray in her hands. She has re-entered. My hands tremble as I take the cup.

'Are you tired?'

I shake my head and take the coffee into the conservatory. 'No, not tired, but it's so rotten that I can't tell you where I've been all this time.'

'You mustn't make too much of an effort. The main thing is that you're back.'

I slowly drink my coffee and look at her. As I look she becomes more and more familiar. Or familiar once again.

'What are you looking at?'

'It's so wonderful to look at you.'

The record switches itself off with a click.

'Shall I turn it over?' she asks.

'No, don't bother,' I say.

'And Wouter. Did you tell him?'

'Only on Wednesday. Until then I just said that you'd gone on a business trip.'

'And at the office?'

'They were sweet. They dropped by every day, and kept my spirits up.'

'But Wouter,' I say. 'How did he react?'

'He's strange. When something bad has happened he shuts himself off. He'll be here any minute.'

'It's odd,' I say. 'I can hear you telling me about it and it's like you're talking about someone else, as though it's a made-up story.'

She looks at me. 'Yesterday we really thought you were dead.' She clenches her hands into fists. 'Christ, I'm so happy!' She gets up and kisses me, hard and fierce; I feel our teeth clash. Yet her kiss doesn't really reach me. Her passion makes me feel a little disconsolate.

I turn my head away. 'There's Wouter.'

First I see the bicycle handlebars moving into the window frame. And then Wouter in a dark blue track-suit. He's had his hair cut, and his skull is close-cropped. I wave, but he ducks as though I'm throwing something at him. Then I realize that he's locking his bike. I want to get up, open the door for him.

'Don't worry,' says Marion. 'He's got a key.'

A boy with a hockey stick comes into the room. He has protruding ears and his upper teeth stick out a little. His face is narrow and he looks at me thoughtfully. Many people say he looks like me. There's no doubt about it. This is Wouter, my son.

'Did you win?' I ask.

He puts the hockey stick in a corner of the room and comes over to us. Marion gets up. 'Come and sit here,' she says. She goes off as though she has something very urgent to do all of a sudden.

Wouter sits down awkwardly opposite me, as though his knees are hurting.

'Where have you been all this time?' His voice is at once insistent and anxious.

I spread my hands in a childish gesture. 'No idea.'

'But you must know where you've been.'

'No,' I say. 'You may find it weird but that's exactly what I don't know.'

He says nothing, looks at the dirt under his nails. Then he looks at me uncertainly.

'Have you forgotten everything then?' he asks in disbelief.

'Perhaps,' I say. 'I'm not even sure of that.'

'But you can't not have been there.'

He's intelligent, Wouter. He's trying to understand what has happened to his father. There has to be a reason for all the suffering his mother has been through in the last ten days, but I can't supply it. It wouldn't surprise me if he gets angry with me in a minute.

'Do you remember that game of Electro we bought for your birthday once?'

He shakes his head.

'About ten years ago. You couldn't read then. You had to put cards with words on them on top of pictures. "Cow" on cow, "barn" on barn. If you got it right and put the plugs in the sockets at the bottom of the box a red light went on. When that happened you clapped your hands with pleasure. Like this, with your hands above your head. To begin with you just played about, but after a while you knew exactly which word belonged with which picture. Infallibly. I don't know if it was really reading, but at any rate you could do it. It certainly looked like it. Don't you remember?'

'No,' says Wouter. 'It's too long ago. I was too young to be able to remember it. But what has that – '

I interrupt him with an understanding nod of my head. 'I know what you're going to ask. But something similar has been happening to me for the past few days. At least that's what it reminds me of most. You see a thing, and you know the word for it, but you can't put the two together any more. They've become separate worlds. I can't explain it any better than that.'

I ought to lie down. I get up and walk over to Marion, who is just putting down the phone. There are tears running down her face.

'I'm going for a nap, I think,' I say.

'Come on.' She takes my hand as though I am a child, as though I'm little Wouter who needs taking to bed.

In the doorway I look round again at my son. He has crossed his legs. Yes, he's like me. My spitting image, in fact.

'Did you win?' I ask.

'Nearly,' he says.

At the top of the stairs I let go of Marion's hand. 'I can find my own way now,' I say.

For a moment I imagine I can hear voices downstairs; a muted conversation which slowly dies away. Then the sinking begins, into the darkness, towards my skates which have been lying on the bottom for so long, waiting for me.

There I go, out on to the silent surface. Alone on the pitch-black ice. On my way. In the distance the silent fringes of reeds. The other side. From left to right, from right to left. The sharp blades singing over the rock-hard ice. And beneath it the dark accompaniment from the depths. Left, right. Right, left. On my way. Further and further, further and further away from me.